THE BUCCANEER DUKE

(A Renegade Royals Novella)

VANESSA KELLY

Dedicated to my readers who loved Antonia Barnett in HIS WICKED REVENGE, and wanted to know what happened to her.

Cover art by Maroli Designs

www.marolidesignservices.com

E-book and print formatting by Web Crafters

www.webcraftersdesign.com

THE BUCCANEER DUKE

Captain Roman Cantrell, illegitimate son of a royal duke, served his country as a ruthless privateer on the high seas. But the war is over and his father orders him home to London to find a respectable wife, one who will help restore his reputation amongst the ton.

But the only woman Roman finds remotely attractive is the opposite of respectable. Antonia Barnett is decidedly unconventional, positively scandalous—and entirely enchanting. Unfortunately, she's also the daughter of his greatest rival, a man who believes that Roman's dangerous past will come back to haunt him.

But troublesome fathers and ruthless enemies are no match for Antonia—as Roman is about to find out…

CHAPTER ONE

"I don't suppose *you* would consider marrying me, would you?" Antonia Barnett asked in a hopeful voice.

"I'd rather throw myself in the Serpentine," said Richard Keane. "You know I'd die a thousand deaths for you, old girl. Getting leg-shackled, however, is out of the question."

She tried to work up a grumpy response, but Richard was her dearest chum, and she'd known him for so long that it was difficult to see anything but friendship between them. Besides, she was no great beauty, small and skinny to the point of angularity. Those characteristics served her well in certain circumstances, yet were decidedly detrimental when casting lures for a mate.

"You could do worse," she said, "especially since I'm rich."

"Confound it, Tony, keep your voice down," Richard hissed, glancing toward the front of the supper box. "My mother would love for us to get riveted. She's like a dog with a bone on the subject. I'll never hear the end of it if you start up again."

Rebecca Keane was sitting nearby with Antonia's mother, eating Vauxhall's paltry excuse for a supper and engaging in animated conversation. Antonia's father, as usual, stood and kept a watchful eye on the occupants of the other boxes and the crowds strolling along the colonnaded walks of the Grove. Papa had never been a fan of Vauxhall Gardens. He was convinced that it was a den of thieves, drunks, rakes, and prostitutes, all scheming to take advantage of respectable women like his wife and daughter.

He wasn't entirely wrong, as Antonia had personally witnessed. But unlike her father, she loved Vauxhall, with its wide avenues and groves of trees glittering in the light of thousands of colorful glass lanterns. If Papa ever found out that she and Richard occasionally snuck off to spend evenings strolling those groves and peeking into secluded grottos, he would have an apoplectic fit.

As far as Antonia was concerned, parents were best kept in the dark about potential areas of conflict. It made life easier for all concerned.

"Our mothers can't hear us," she replied. "Not over the din of the orchestra. Why they must play an endless stream of military marches is beyond me. I can barely hear myself think."

"They're practicing for next week's celebrations to commemorate our great victory at Waterloo."

Antonia scoffed. "The Prince Regent is no doubt more concerned with celebrating his birthday than the end of the war. If there's anything Prinny loves it's a good party."

The next few weeks would see a veritable orgy of balls, concerts, and fireworks to honor both the defeat of Napoleon and the Regent's birthday. Many of the events would be held at Vauxhall Gardens. Like Prinny himself, the festivities were bound to be overblown, gaudy, and ridiculously extravagant.

The fact that they would undoubtedly be a great deal of fun too meant Antonia had every intention of attending as many as she could, even if it meant telling a few white lies to her parents. Top on her list was the prizefight rumored to take place a few days after the masked ball. While such fights were thoroughly illegal and no place for a lady that simply made her all the more determined to attend—although certainly not as a lady.

"Maybe you'll meet some new suitors during the celebrations," Richard said. "Bound to be some fellow who will take a shine to you."

"Richard, I've been on the Marriage Mart for three years, and we all know I'm an abject failure. It would take a miracle of monumental proportions to change that."

Her friend's gaze warmed with sympathy. "Is that why you came up with that cracked brain idea to marry me?"

"You must admit it would solve more than a few problems. Papa would stop worrying about me, and your mother would be deliriously happy. We could eventually run Nightingale Trading together, and we'd be as rich as King Solomon."

"You mean you'd be rich as Solomon. My father is a minority partner, remember?"

"No matter. As my husband, you'd control my fortune. One day you'd be the head of everything."

Everything would include one of the most influential trading companies in England. Under normal circumstances, Antonia should be a considerable prize as a result. Her circumstances, however, were anything but normal.

"Sorry, old gal, it's still not enough to tempt me," Richard said. "Besides, you'd bully me unmercifully. We both know you have a better head for business than I do."

"Nonsense, you're very good with numbers, just like your father. You'd be splendid running Nightingale Trading."

"Not as splendid as you. And your father would make me walk the plank before he allowed us to marry. Only a rich aristocrat will do for his darling daughter, as he's made abundantly clear."

"Yes, and look how well it's worked out," she said gloomily. "It'll be a miracle if anyone wants to marry me after last week's incident."

"Were you talking about marriage, my dear?" interjected Mrs. Keane, who'd obviously been eavesdropping. She smiled archly at Antonia's mother. "I have said a thousand times that my son and your daughter would make the perfect match. After all, they are such good friends."

"Yes, so good they are like brother and sister," Mamma replied with a twinkle in her beautiful blue eyes.

"True enough, Mrs. Barnett," Richard said with a grateful smile. "And we'd probably kill each other after a week, anyway, so there's that."

"Nonsense," huffed Mrs. Keane. "Everyone knows friendship is the best foundation for marriage. Antonia and you are well-suited in all respects."

Antonia's father had been lounging against a railing at the front of the box, but Mrs. Keane's brassy voice caught his attention. "We've discussed this more than once, Rebecca. As estimable as Richard is, he and Antonia are *not* suited for each other."

Richard gave a dramatic shudder. "Can't think of anything more dismal, actually."

"Richard Keane!" his mother exclaimed. "What a terrible thing to say about your dearest friend."

"He's probably right, Mrs. Keane," Antonia said, wrinkling her nose. "And his opinion is generally shared by everyone on the Marriage Mart. I suspect I'm doomed for spinsterhood."

"Nonsense, darling," Mamma said. "Everyone thinks you're lovely."

"And if they don't, they'll have me to answer to," Papa said in a stern tone.

Antonia's father was a tall, broad-shouldered man in his early forties. Rugged and imposing, his over-protective manner towards his only child—while endearing—was yet another impediment to her quest to find a suitable husband.

"I believe Lord Totten discovered that when you tossed him into the pond at Green Park," she said.

"I didn't toss him," Papa said in a defensive tone. "I just gave him a little push. He insulted you, and I won't have that."

The viscount had simply made a veiled reference to Antonia's eye color, an unusual golden-amber and the exact match of her father's. Normally, one might take such a remark as a compliment. And given that she was rather ordinary looking, they counted as her best feature.

But though she'd inherited Papa's eyes, he was technically her stepfather. Antonia's parents had been childhood sweethearts and then young lovers until tragically separated by unfeeling relatives. Papa had been thrown out on his ear without a shilling, while Mamma had been hastily pushed into marriage with a wealthy baronet. Convinced the love of his life had abandoned him, Papa had set sail for the Americas, where he'd made his fortune in shipping.

Mamma had been forced to pretend she'd become pregnant by her new husband, not Anthony Barnett. Eventually, Sir Richard Paget had deduced Antonia was another man's child. While he'd been decent enough to go along with the charade until he died, Sir Richard had never shown a scrap of affection to either his wife or Antonia.

When she was a little girl, she had always wondered why her father didn't like her, and she'd never been able to shake the sensation that the fault rested with her.

A few short weeks after her twelfth birthday, Captain Anthony Barnett returned to London, seeking revenge against the woman he was convinced had betrayed him. To say he'd been stunned when he first set eyes on Antonia was an understatement. It had been a shock for her, too. All the questions of her life had been answered in the moment when she gazed into the eyes of the man who was obviously her real father.

Matters had been fraught for a day or two, but eventually Papa accepted that Mamma had been trying to protect everyone by her deception. They had married almost immediately, and Papa had adopted Antonia. To avoid scandal, they still pretended he was only her stepfather, and the polite world mostly went along with the fiction.

After all, Papa was *very* rich.

But only a particularly credulous person could fail to notice that they shared the same unusual eye color, not to mention, for all intents and purposes, a first name. It had the unfortunate effect of making Antonia less than respectable, and sometimes even the object of unfeeling gossip. She only gave a fig when Papa did something like tossing a would-be suitor into a pond.

"Lord Totten was just making an observation," she said.

"One that has been made numerous times over the years," Mamma reminded him. "I would think you'd be used to it by now, Anthony."

"I will never grow used to anyone insulting my daughter. Or you, for that matter," he said, taking his wife's hand. "Anyone who does will regret it."

When he gallantly kissed the inside of her wrist, Mamma blushed. Mrs. Keane giggled and fluttered her handkerchief like a debutante. Although Antonia rolled her eyes, it was hard not to admire her parents. They were like characters out of a novel—larger than life, with a love to match.

"Lord Totten certainly came to regret it," she said.

"He caught a dreadful cold," Mamma said ruefully. "His poor mother told me it was quite a violent taking."

Antonia sighed. She'd rather liked Lord Totten, despite his occasionally smirking attitude. At least he made an effort to speak with her.

"That's ridiculous," her father protested. "He barely got wet."

"He got soaked. The point is, Papa, if you keep threatening the few suitors I have, I'll be an old maid in no time."

She had yet to receive a decent offer in three years. There'd been a few young men who'd proposed, but it was clear they simply wanted her fortune. Antonia would never be so desperate as to accept an offer from a man whose only interest was in the state of her purse, not the state of her heart.

"I only threaten the ones who don't respect you," Papa said. "Nor am I responsible for the fact that most men are buffoons. You are exceedingly smart and nice, and you're the prettiest girl in London. You take after your mother, so it's no wonder."

Antonia wasn't a patch on her gorgeous mother. Still, Papa believed every word he said. It was terribly sweet of him, of course, but also painful because she was letting him down.

Richard poked her in the arm. "He's right, Tony. After all, you're lots of fun, and you never nag a fellow. You'll make a splendid wife."

"Just not for you," she joked. "Or did I get that wrong?"

Mrs. Keane leapt in like an acrobat. "Of course my son would love to marry you. Just name the day, my dear."

"Confound it," Richard muttered.

"I repeat, Antonia and Richard do not suit," Papa said to Mrs. Keane. "And your husband agrees with me."

The older woman snorted. "As if Simon would ever disagree with anything you said. You quite dominate him."

"I do nothing of the sort. I simply explain things in a rational manner, and then Simon agrees with me."

They *all* rolled their eyes. Papa and Mr. Keane were partners and great friends, but no one doubted who ruled the roost at Nightingale Trading. Antonia's father was a force of nature, always convinced he knew best. The fact that he was usually correct didn't make the characteristic any less annoying.

Mamma tapped him on the arm. "Dearest, there's Mr. Woods. Did you not say the other day that you needed to speak with him?"

Much to everyone's relief, her intervention worked.

"I do. Thank you for the reminder," Papa said, waving to his friend.

He was soon engaged in business discussions with Mr. Woods, while Mamma and Mrs. Keane resumed their chat about the latest fashions.

Richard pulled out a handkerchief and wiped his brow. "Crisis averted. Don't joke about us getting married, Tony. It's not worth it."

Antonia shook her head. "I'm going to have to do something about Papa. He simply won't give up trying to marry me off, and he's awful at it. Nothing Mamma and I say makes a difference."

"Because it's become a matter of pride for him."

"His or mine?"

He grinned. "His, obviously. You don't have any pride. Your father, however, won't be satisfied with anything less than a duke for you."

"I'd be lucky to snag a knight, given the gossip about my birth and the fact that Papa is a merchant."

"True, but he's a filthy rich merchant. That has to count for something."

"Not so far."

"Oh, I don't know. There's a fellow who seems very interested in you. He's been staring like anything for the last several minutes."

Antonia couldn't help perking up. "Really?"

"He's just to the left, first box over."

The supper boxes at Vauxhall lined three sides of the Grove. Papa had managed to secure one near the end of a row, giving them a good vantage point for watching the festivities. Unfortunately, the crowd now milling about in front of the orchestra pavilion partly obstructed her view, forcing Antonia to crane sideways around her mother to see.

When she saw what Richard meant, she almost toppled over in shock.

There *was* a man staring at her, and with an intensity she felt in the pit of her stomach. He was big and broad-shouldered and looked rather menacing, even though he lounged informally, one booted foot propped up on the rail in front of him. His hair was dark and cut ruthlessly short, and a scar ran down the side of his face. Starkly garbed in unadorned black, but for a snowy white cravat and a gold hoop that dangled from one ear, he resembled nothing so much as a pirate. A dramatically handsome, even elegant, pirate.

She hastily retreated, her heart banging like mad. "If he's staring at me in particular, it's not with admiration. He looks like he wants to hang me from the nearest yardarm."

Richard leaned forward to take another look. "That's not how I would describe it."

She frowned. "Then how would you describe it?"

"If you don't know, I'm not going to tell you."

"You are so annoying. Do you have any idea who he is?"

"Can't say that I do. He's not the sort I would likely forget."

"Indeed not. He looks like a buccaneer."

"Or a highwayman."

"Maybe it's a costume, and he got the dates mixed up," she said. "The masked ball isn't until later in the week."

Richard snorted. "Any self-respecting man would go home and change rather than prance around dressed up like a confounded pirate."

She peeked out again. The man was still staring at her with unnerving intent. Still, it was rather exciting. Men usually only stared at her if she'd done something clumsy or they were gossiping about her murky parentage.

Antonia tapped her mother's shoulder. "Do you know why that gentleman is staring at us?"

Mamma gave her a distracted glance. "I imagine it's because you look especially pretty tonight, my dear."

Her father, having just said farewell to Mr. Woods, turned with a concerned expression. "Is someone bothering you, pet? Point him out this instant."

"No one is bothering me. I simply wondered about that man in the box at the end of the row. He seems quite interested in me. Um, in us, I mean."

"Where exactly—" Her father fell silent as he stared at the mysterious gentleman.

"Do you know him?" Antonia prompted.

"Yes, and he's not staring at you," Papa said. "He's staring at me."

"Oh. That's a relief, I suppose. I see he's sitting with Mr. Steele. You know him, do you not?"

Her father's sharp gaze whipped back to her. "Antonia, how do you know Steele?"

She mentally winced, since she wasn't supposed to know people like Griffin Steele. Not that she personally knew the former crime lord, but she'd seen him more than once at Vauxhall during her secret excursions with Richard.

"I saw him at Gunter's a few weeks ago. He was with his wife, having ices." That, at least, was the truth. "Richard pointed him out to me," she added, trying to sound innocent.

Papa frowned. "And how does Richard know who he is?"

Richard's eyes grew round. "Ah…"

"Goodness, everyone knows Mr. Steele," Mamma said, coming to their rescue. "He's entirely respectable now that he's married."

"That is a matter of opinion," Papa said. "I certainly don't see him as fit company for our daughter, as is evidenced by the confounded blighter who's with him."

"And exactly who *is* the, er, blighter?" Antonia asked. "And why is he staring at you with such a ferocious expression?"

"Probably because he wants to gut me. And that is exactly what I wish to do to him." With that trenchant remark, her father stalked out and headed toward Mr. Steele's box.

Mamma let out a long-suffering sigh. "That dramatic-looking man must be one of your father's business rivals."

"If he is, they're certainly not friendly rivals," Antonia said.

As one of the most successful traders in England, Papa had plenty of competitors and even a few outright enemies. He was more than capable of handling anyone who challenged him, but this man seemed different.

Dangerous.

Mrs. Keane looked worried. "Anthony appears to be extremely annoyed. I do hope they don't get into a fight."

Mamma rose from the table. "I'm sure it's all a misunderstanding. In any case, Anthony would never start a brawl in public—especially after I remind him of that."

"I'll go, Mamma," Antonia said, jumping up.

"Certainly not." Her mother made a grab for her.

Antonia deftly evaded her. "Don't worry. I won't start any brawls, either."

Unless, that is, the mystery man threatened her father. Then he'd have Antonia Barnett to deal with, too.

***

Roman Cantrell pointed a finger at Griffin's cheek. "That is the most paltry excuse for a scar I have ever seen. Besides, you got yours falling out of a tree when you were a brat in short pants. I got mine in a knife fight off the Barbary Coast."

"You may have a better scar, but my tattoo is miles better than yours," his cousin said as he replenished Roman's glass with wine.

"How the hell do you know what my tattoo looks like?"

"Doesn't matter. I know mine is better."

Roman snorted his disdain. He'd gotten his tattoo in Tripoli, and it had hurt like hell.

"Would you like to see?" Griffin asked. "I'll show mine if you show yours."

"Don't make me ill. Besides, your wife would look askance if we stripped in public."

"It wouldn't be the most outrageous thing I've ever done in front of Justine."

"I can believe it." Roman was still amazed that Griffin had convinced a lovely, decent woman like Justine Brightmore to marry him. In fact, he found it hard to believe his cousin had managed to get himself both leg-shackled *and* reformed. But if Griffin could do it, a man whose reputation was far worse than his, perhaps there was hope for Roman after all.

That's what his father, the Duke of Clarence, was hoping. Unfortunately, respectable society misses either turned pale with fright as soon as Roman talked to them, or their mothers dragged them away, as if terrified he'd ravish them in the middle of a ballroom.

So far, he hadn't been tempted to ravish anyone. Every single girl he'd met since returning to England had bored him silly.

"Speaking of outrageous," Griffin said, "I hope you're not planning to challenge Captain Barnett to a duel. If you keep staring at his family so pointedly, that's the likely outcome. He's very protective of them, especially his stepdaughter."

Seven years older than Roman, Barnett was still a big, imposing man in his prime. But he wasn't as big as Roman, or as ruthless. Barnett had principles, whereas Roman had learned long ago that loyalty and honor could bite you in the arse if you weren't careful.

"I have no interest in his daughter," he said. "In case you've failed to notice, she has all the appeal of a lamp post. I would have mistaken her for a boy if not for the dress and that pile of hair on her head."

Griffin chuckled. "Truer than you know."

"What's that supposed to mean?"

"Ah, I see our little staring contest has prompted the good captain to head this way, which I presume was your intent. Again, I feel compelled to reiterate my concerns about public brawling. Justine and my mother will be returning any moment, and neither will take it kindly if they stumble into impromptu fisticuffs."

Roman smiled with satisfaction as Barnett strode toward them, murder in his gaze. Having it out with his chief rival was a priority, and a chance encounter in Vauxhall was perfectly acceptable. Barnett needed to hear Roman's warning loud and clear and it wouldn't hurt to have witnesses.

"I only resort to physical violence when absolutely necessary, Griffin. I merely wish to issue Barnett a polite warning about interfering in my business."

"I'm sure it will be very polite."

Griffin rose to his feet as Barnett stalked up to their box. Roman, however, made a point of staying where he was—boots propped up on the rail, wineglass dangling in his hand. As tough as he was, Barnett was not a thug. He'd fought his way to the top of a dangerous profession using his wits and his fists, but he was still a gentleman.

Roman, however, wasn't a gentleman, despite his royal blood. The wary reaction of the *ton* to his reappearance among their ranks made that as clear as a sunrise over the South China Sea.

Barnett's glare remained lethal. "If you have something to say to me, Cantrell, then say it. Do not send threatening looks my way, or stare my wife and daughter out of countenance."

"But they don't seem the slightest bit discomposed by my admiring glances," Roman said. "Quite the opposite."

That was hardly true. Mrs. Barnett had barely glanced at him, but the daughter had stared at him with an expression torn between fascination and horror. At least she hadn't pulled out her smelling salts, like several young ladies he'd met.

"My family is off limits," Barnett said. "Don't even think about exacting retribution through them, or you will find yourself at the bottom of the Thames."

Roman snorted. "I'm quaking in my boots."

When the captain's hands curled into fists, Griffin heaved a sigh. "Sir, as much as my cousin deserves it, I beg you to refrain from punching him. The pleasures of Vauxhall may seem tame compared to your exciting lives on the high seas, but I hardly think the ladies will be pleased by an impromptu prizefight."

Barnett shot Griffin an irritated look. "I have no intention of starting a brawl, not that it's any business of yours. I'll thank you to stay out of it."

"I beg to differ. I take any threat to Captain Cantrell as a threat to me."

Coming from Griffin Steele, that sort of statement would normally have had grown men pissing down their legs.

Not Barnett. "That has me quaking in my boots, it does," he mocked. "You're as bad as Cantrell, so ask me if I care about your opinion."

As enjoyable as it was for Roman to listen to his cousin spar with his rival, it was time to get down to business. He was about to do just that when the sight of a small figure dashing toward them with single-minded determination caught his eye. Antonia Barnett apparently had no trouble shoving men twice her size out of the way.

"I hate to interrupt your splendid tirade," Roman said as he finally rose, "but it seems your stepdaughter is about to join us."

Miss Barnett swanned up with a challenging smile that dared anyone to object to her presence. For such a petite thing, she seemed to have a great deal of brass, especially in the face of her father's disapproving glower.

"Antonia, why are you marching about without an escort? You know I hate that," Barnett snapped. "Please return to our box immediately."

She peered at him, as if perplexed. "That request makes no sense, Papa. You just said I shouldn't be walking about without an escort."

"That is simply a neat bit of sophistry, and you know it," her father sternly replied.

The girl laughed. The sound, full-throated and warm, was nothing like the polite titter society misses employed to express amusement.

"I'm just teasing, Papa," she said, pressing Barnett's arm. "You know I'm perfectly safe in the Grove, especially with you only a few boxes away. In any case, Mamma sent me to fetch you. She's afraid you might get into a disagreement with your, er, friends, and cause a scene that would distress the ladies."

"Good God," her father muttered.

"In the interest of peace," Griffin said with a smile, "allow me to make the introductions. I am Griffin Steele, and this is my cousin, Captain Roman Cantrell."

Miss Barnett dipped into a curtsy. "It's a pleasure to meet you, Mr. Steele." Then she turned to Roman, squarely meeting his gaze for the first time. "And you, Captain Cantrell. I'm honored to make your acquaintance."

For a moment, Roman thought he was seeing things. In the light of hundreds of lanterns hanging from the trees, she seemed to shimmer like a fairy, half in and half out of the world of man. Her thick hair gleamed like moonlight, and her spangled yellow dress coasted over the gentle curves of her lithe figure, glittering with her every movement. Her smile was charmingly fey, as if she alone were privy to a splendid joke.

But it was the eyes that truly gave him a jolt. Of rich, honeyed amber, they were framed with lashes so lavish her eyes appeared lined with kohl. Staring into that gaze was like looking at sunshine.

And then it hit him. The girl had inherited those eyes from Barnett, the man who claimed to be her stepfather. That gaze—and her forthright manner—testified to Barnett blood running strong and true.

From her resigned sigh, it was obvious she was used to people reaching that conclusion. Roman couldn't help but feel a twinge of sympathy, since he understood how difficult it was to pretend to be something you weren't.

"What the devil is wrong with you, Cantrell?" Barnett growled. "The least you could do is respond to the poor girl instead of gaping at her like an idiot."

"Damnation, Barnett," Roman said. "I thought you didn't want me even talking to your precious little darling."

"I don't, but she's taken the matter out of my hands. And you will refrain from using foul language in her presence."

Antonia turned her big, innocent-looking eyes on her father. "Papa, you frequently swear in my presence at the office."

"I do not."

"Of course you do. In fact, you made me vow never to tell Mamma, remember?"

He grimaced. "Oh, hell. Don't say anything or we'll both be in for it."

"It is our little secret," his daughter said in a solemn voice.

Barnett's aggrieved huff spoke volumes about their relationship. Roman had to admit it was surprisingly entertaining to see the gruff trader tied up in knots by a slip of a girl.

"Do you often visit your father's offices?" Griffin asked in an amused voice. "Wapping is not exactly a stroll in Mayfair."

The captain bristled. "Are you suggesting I don't know how to protect my own child?"

"Not at all," Griffin said. "In fact, I would commend you for being so open-minded a parent."

"No one in Wapping would dare touch me," Antonia said. "They know Papa would cut their hearts out and toss their bodies into the river."

Barnett looked about to have an apoplectic fit. Roman found himself liking Miss Barnett more by the minute.

"And do you enjoy visiting your father's office?" he asked.

"I do," she said. "I have a head for numbers and often help with the ledgers."

"That's a rather unusual pastime for a young lady."

She hesitated a fraction too long. "It's odd of me, I know."

"There's nothing odd about you, my dear." Barnett narrowed his gaze on Roman. "Surely you're not suggesting there's something wrong with a young woman having a brain."

"On the contrary. There's nothing more appalling than a stupid woman."

"Except a stupid man," Antonia said.

"Oh, well done," murmured Griffin.

Roman had to swallow a chuckle. "I'm sure you're a great help to your father. God knows he could use it."

He meant it as both a jest and a compliment, but her gaze sparked with disapproval. Clearly, she was very protective of Barnett, as he was of her.

"Women often have better heads for business," Griffin smoothly interjected. "Take my mother. She's been successfully running her charitable institution for years."

Antonia rewarded Griffin with a warm smile. It turned her elfin features, which were too sharp and clever to be deemed conventionally pretty, into something approaching beauty. Roman wondered what it would be like to have such a smile directed at him.

"I've heard about Lady Hunter's wonderful charity for girls and their babies," she said. "I wish I could be so useful."

"You do lots of useful things," her father said gruffly. "You take care of your mother and me, for one."

"Thank you, Papa, but that hardly compares to Lady Hunter's estimable work."

"Perhaps you'd like to visit her someday," Griffin said. "She's established just outside the city, in Camberwell."

Barnett scowled. "That won't be—"

"I would love that," Antonia enthused. "If you're certain Lady Hunter wouldn't mind."

"Of course not, but you can ask her yourself. She and my wife are just returning from a stroll around the Grove."

"Are you gossiping about us, my son?" said Chloe Hunter a moment later as she stepped up to the box. "I swear my ears are burning."

"No, just giving you compliments, Mother. Do you know Captain Barnett and his daughter, Miss Antonia Barnett?"

Roman's aunt gave the pair a gracious smile. "No, but I believe my husband knows the captain. Would you and Miss Barnett care to join us, sir?"

"Thank you, but we have no wish to inconvenience you," Barnett said stiffly. He gave a short bow and began to pull his daughter away.

Justine put out a quick hand. "I believe we saw you last week at Gunter's, Miss Barnett. Did we not?"

"You did, Mrs. Steele," Antonia said. "I was there with a friend."

"Ah, yes, a very nice looking young man, as I recall."

Roman was surprised to realize he didn't like the idea of Miss Antonia Barnett spending time with nice looking young men.

"Richard Keane," Griffin supplied. "Son of Captain Barnett's partner."

"Do you know everyone in this blasted town?" Barnett groused.

"It's an annoying characteristic, isn't it?" Justine said. "I can never tell my husband anything he doesn't seem to already know."

"It's a burden, being right all the time," Griffin said.

"How awful for you," Barnett replied. "And, now, if you'll excuse us…"

"I do believe Miss Barnett wished to ask me something," Chloe interrupted.

The girl brightened. "Yes, please. I was wondering if you could tell me about your charity."

"I should be happy to," Chloe said. "Won't you join us in our box? We have more than enough room."

Barnett looked appalled.

"Yes, plenty of room," said Roman with malicious pleasure. "And you should join us too, Barnett. I'm sure we could find something to talk about."

"I think not. Come along, Antonia."

Barnett's daughter adopted a comically woeful expression. "Must we go, Papa? I truly would like to speak to Lady Hunter."

"We promise to take good care of her, Captain Barnett," Justine said with gentle reassurance.

"And we won't corrupt her in the slightest," Griffin added. "Ouch," he said when his mother elbowed him.

"Your daughter will be perfectly safe with me, Captain," Chloe said. "You have my word."

Barnett now had no way to refuse without causing insult, and no one in his right mind insulted Lady Hunter. After all, she was the wife of Dominic Hunter, one of the most powerful and well-regarded men in the *ton*.

Barnett gave in fairly graciously. "That's very kind of you, ma'am." Then he narrowed his gaze on his daughter, and she narrowed an identical gaze right back at him. "Antonia, I will expect you back in our box in thirty minutes, or I will fetch you myself. Is that clear?"

"Yes, Papa," she said in a dutiful voice that fooled exactly no one—including Barnett, from his quiet snort.

When Antonia stretched up on her tiptoes to kiss his cheek, the man's stern features softened with a vulnerability Roman had never seen in him. Father and daughter were clearly thick as thieves.

Barnett shot a warning glance his way. "I will be talking to you soon, Cantrell."

Roman flashed him a toothy smile. "I will wait with breathless anticipation, my dear sir."

The captain pivoted on his boot heel and stalked back through the crowd.

Antonia flashed Roman an irritated glance. "I wish you wouldn't do that."

"What?"

"Tease my father."

"But he makes it so easy."

She gave him a shoulder as she accepted Griffin's hand-up onto the platform. Griffin relinquished his seat, joining his wife on the other side of the box and leaving Antonia between Chloe and Roman.

Even though she was turned away from him, Roman didn't mind. He could admire her slender neck, exposed by the upsweep of moonlit-blond hair arranged in a shimmering tumble on the crown of her head. She also had a graceful back, a narrow waist, and a gentle yet enticing curve to her hips. Antonia might be petite, but she was far from being a lamppost. In fact, she possessed an understated femininity he found surprisingly appealing, even without the generous curves he normally preferred.

In fact, so appealing that there was a decided tightness in his breeches, an odd and alarming realization. She was Barnett's daughter, for God's sake, and the last girl who should stir his desire.

He glanced over to Barnett's supper box. As he could have predicted, his rival was glaring daggers at him. If anything could deflate a burgeoning erection, the ice in Barnett's gaze was it.

Roman let his eyes wander over the crowd that fluttered like demented moths under the lamp-lighted trees. After months at sea—and after the hard years of the war—he'd been looking forward to a new life in London. He'd always been good at his work, as good as anyone who commanded a ship. But that didn't mean he loved it. His life had been thrust upon him by birth and circumstances beyond his control. He'd accomplished much, coming home from war with a trading company well on its way to rivaling more established outfits. And with his royal father's help, Roman would be able to secure even bigger contracts and more ships.

Yes, he was more than ready to leave life on the high seas behind. More than ready to find a highborn wife and settle down to a self-satisfied existence like the rest of the *ton*. He'd earned it, by God, with blood and treasure. It was time for the world to pay up.

The one small problem with his plan was that life on dry land was proving to be exceedingly dull.

A poke on the arm pulled him out of his ruminations. He glanced sideways to see Antonia regarding him with annoyance.

"Miss Barnett, is there something you want, or do you simply enjoy jabbing holes in a man's sleeve?"

"It seemed the most expedient way to get your attention. I've spoken to you twice already, but you ignored me. As usual," she ended on a mutter.

He frowned. "Miss Barnett, how can I ignore you *as usual* if we've only just met?"

"Sorry. It's just that most gentlemen have a tendency to overlook me. When they're not calling me odd."

He studied the blush that colored her high cheekbones. She was very pretty when one took the time to look. Aside from the spectacular eyes, she had a charming, tip-tilted nose and a full, rosebud mouth made for smiles and kisses.

"You're rather blunt," Roman said. "Some people might think that odd in a young lady."

"I do try to control myself, but my thoughts somehow spring out at the most inconvenient times." She scrunched her nose. "I can't keep count of all the people I've offended, when I should have ignored them instead."

Ignored the gossip and insults, she meant. Illegitimacy was a heavy burden, doubly so for a gently bred and clearly sensitive young woman like Antonia.

"I keep a chart," he said. "That way I can track how many people I've rubbed the wrong way. It's quite handy when I can't recall why someone is snubbing me."

Her golden eyes filled with laughter. "That's an excellent idea. If nothing else, it might prevent me from wasting a good insult on a person I've already irritated."

"Exactly. It's best to keep one's disparaging comments as fresh as possible."

"You're very good at that, if Papa's behavior is any indication."

"I'm quite well known for it. Now, what is it you wished to ask me when you were abusing my sleeve a few moments ago?"

She pursed her mouth, as if reconsidering, then gave a tiny shrug. "I'd like to know why you hate my father."

He raised his eyebrows. "Blunt doesn't begin to cover it."

She held his gaze with a touch of defiance.

"For the record," he finally said, "I do not hate your father."

Not much, anyway.

Now it was her turn to raise her eyebrows. "He certainly seems to hate you. And since my father is a very fair man, I have to believe there's a good reason for it."

"Perhaps I have given him cause over the years, although it's nothing personal, I assure you. Our dealings are entirely business related. During the war, I may have outbid him on one or two contracts that he particularly wanted."

She nodded. "Papa is extremely competitive."

"So am I."

"I suppose that would explain it. It seems rather silly, though. Papa is very wealthy, and I suspect you're fairly plump in the pocket, too. You certainly look it."

When her interested gaze flickered over his body, he felt a surge of desire and had to clear his throat before answering. "It's the nature of business. One always seeks to put one's rivals in the ground."

Her scowl was sudden and fierce. "I hope you're joking."

"I was speaking metaphorically, of course."

"My father is very good at what he does, as those who try to *put him in the ground* invariably find out."

Roman simply shrugged.

"And how many ships do you own?" she asked.

"Three."

"My father owns ten," she said smugly.

When Roman laughed, she gave him a reluctant smile.

"Are you staying in town, or will you soon set off again?" she asked.

It was a polite enquiry, but he could tell she was fishing. "I'll be running my business in London from now on. In fact, I'm looking for office and warehouse space in Wapping."

He didn't normally discuss his business affairs with society misses. However, since Antonia would likely transmit some of the details of their conversation back to her father, it occurred to him that she could be a useful conduit of information.

He could think of additional ways that a relationship with her might prove fruitful and pleasurable, but it was best to ignore those promptings.

"Huh," she said. "So I imagine we might be running into each other on occasion. Socially, I mean."

"Probably. I'll be looking for a wife on the Marriage Mart, so perhaps you could give me some suggestions."

"Why would I do that?" she said, sounding a bit flustered. "It would be entirely inappropriate for us to even discuss such a thing, as I'm sure you know."

Her sudden retreat behind social niceties was amusing. "You're right," he said. "Forget I asked. I simply thought you might have some suggestions about how to make myself more attractive to genteel young ladies such as yourself."

Antonia scoffed. "I hardly think you'll have any trouble in that regard, sir."

Ah. How interesting.

"Sadly, my father does not agree. He thinks I'm making a hash of it," Roman said, flashing his most charming smile.

It apparently did the trick because she smiled back. "Perhaps he and Papa can get together and compare notes. Would my father know him?"

"I would think so. He's the Duke of Clarence."

She gazed blankly at him for a moment. "The Duke of Clarence? You mean the *royal* duke?"

"None other."

Her blank stare turned into disbelief. "Really?"

What was the bloody problem? He hardly expected her, of all people, to object to his parentage, especially since his breeding was a damn sight better than hers—not that he gave a tinker's damn about that sort of thing. He simply couldn't abide the notion that Antonia would be as disapproving of him as every other girl in the *ton*.

"Miss Barnett, I didn't realize you were hard of hearing," he said sarcastically.

When she flinched, he felt like a complete rotter.

"I apologize," he said. "That was unforgivably rude of me."

"No…no, I'm the one who's being rude. It's just, oh, never mind." She clambered awkwardly to her feet. "I must go before Papa comes to fetch me. That would not be a good thing, I assure you. Goodbye, Captain Cantrell. It was a pleasure to meet you."

Apparently not, Roman thought with irritation as she made her escape.

Chloe turned to him with a frown. "What did you say to frighten the poor girl?"

"I have no idea."

"He probably just glowered at her," Griffin said. "That's usually enough to send the girls screaming from the room."

"Thank you for that vote of support," Roman replied.

"I'm sure you did no such thing, did you?" Chloe said, patting his arm.

"It doesn't matter."

And it shouldn't. For a few minutes, he'd thought Antonia Barnett was different from the girls his father had tried to foist on him. He'd thought her brave and funny. Odd, yes, but that was somehow part of her charm.

It was a disappointing to know he'd been wrong about a woman. Again.

CHAPTER TWO

Vauxhall was utterly mobbed, as the official celebrations of the Regent's birthday had kicked off with a masked ball. The supper boxes were full to bursting, and thousands of costumed festivalgoers strolled along the walks and through the groves. It was a splendid opportunity for pickpockets, thieves, and prostitutes, and Roman had little doubt London's criminal class was hard at work. Too bad he hadn't thought to stow a pistol inside the sash of his costume, just to be on the safe side.

Propping a shoulder against a tree near the Prince Regent's special supper box, Roman settled in to watch his royal relatives comport themselves with their usual absence of dignity. His uncle, the future King of England, looked particularly ridiculous, swathed in an expansive gold toga with a wreath of laurels circling his head. Meanwhile, Cumberland was clomping around in bits of old armor, and York had costumed himself as a gladiator. Roman was happy to see that his father had garbed himself with a bit more dignity than his three brothers, sporting the costume of a British sailor.

He snatched a wineglass from one of the purple-coated waiters, forestalling the man's objection by flipping him a crown. The food served in the Gardens was generally an abomination, but at least the wine was topnotch. Not that he had any intention of joining his family for supper in the Regent's box, despite his father's pointed suggestion that he do so. Clarence would simply start nagging again about his son's failure to secure a suitable bride, and Roman needed no more reminders of that.

Even Antonia Barnett, who was not exactly the belle of the ball, wanted nothing to do with him.

When a finger jabbed his bicep, he almost spilled his drink.

"What the devil?" he growled.

Roman turned to face what appeared to be a fairy. She wore a pair of spangled wings, a gauzy silver dress, and carried a beribboned wand. Behind a glittering mask, Antonia Barnett waited for him to acknowledge her.

"Miss Barnett, do you enjoy poking defenseless men?" he asked.

"Only when necessary. And you are hardly defenseless."

"What are you doing here?"

"I'm attending the masked ball, just like you." Her tone suggested he was an imbecile.

"I mean, what are you doing accosting *me*?"

"I wished to speak with you." Her mouth tilted down. "And how did you know it was me in this silly outfit?"

Roman would have known her anywhere. She might be rather a little thing, easily passed over at first glance, but she carried herself with unconscious grace. Add in those amazing eyes and hair that glowed like moonlight, and Antonia Barnett was unforgettable.

"I'm so observant that I also instantly deduced you're wandering about by yourself again. Does your father know you're here?"

"I'm with my friend, Mr. Keane, and his parents."

Roman made a show of looking around. "And did they garb themselves in cloaks of invisibility as their disguise?"

"Don't be so silly. Richard is just over there by that pillar, speaking with some friends. He's the Egyptian pharaoh."

"He looks ridiculous." Roman wasn't sure if he disapproved because of the idiot's historically absurd headdress, or the fact that Keane and Antonia were on a first-name basis.

"I said the same thing. Richard was quite offended by my assessment," she said dryly.

"That's no way to treat a devoted swain, Miss Barnett," he said, trying not to laugh.

"Sadly, I do not have any swains. At least not at the moment," she added hastily.

"Hardly surprising. Your father makes a habit of tossing them into the nearest body of water."

"I suppose everyone's heard about that little incident by now."

"I'm afraid so. And knowing your father, I shouldn't be surprised if a bevy of your suitors is currently reposing at the bottom of the Thames."

She starched up. "That is certainly not true."

Roman was about to apologize when she held up an imperious hand. "Never the Thames. Papa only tosses my suitors into the very best bodies of water. Nothing is too good for his darling daughter."

She was absurd—and charming.

"So the pharaonic Mr. Keane is not a suitor."

"No. He's my best friend, actually."

"If he's such a good friend, why isn't he taking better care of you?"

Her fairy wings all but quivered with indignation. "I do not need anyone looking after me, Captain Cantrell."

"I suspect your father would not agree."

"Papa tends to be a bit over-protective, as you may have noticed."

Roman couldn't blame her father at all. When he took in her delicate figure, garbed in a costume that was too enticing, he couldn't believe any man in his right mind would let her wander around on her own—especially not at a place like Vauxhall, where any number of dangers lurked.

"Does your father even know you're here tonight?"

"Of course he does."

"I'm surprised he approved of that outfit. Who are you supposed to be, anyway?"

"Titania, queen of the fairies." She flapped her wand. "I know I look almost as ridiculous as Richard. But it was Mamma's idea, so I couldn't really say no."

In fact, the outfit suited her perfectly. Creamy-colored silk crisscrossed her bodice, highlighting the swell of her small but prettily shaped breasts. The fabric nipped in at her narrow waist, and then belled out in gauzy skirts covered in spangles. Puffy sleeves, delicate wings, and a mask of silver lace completed the picture. Under the soft lights of the Grove it would be easy to mistake her for one of the fey folk, a shimmering creature too ethereal for the mundane world of men.

"Ridiculous is not how I would describe you," he said.

"Oh, no? How would you describe me, then?" she asked softly.

"Lovely, and exactly as a fairy queen should look."

Though she ducked her head, as if embarrassed, he caught her pleased little smile. "I did have another costume in mind, but Mamma put her foot down. I wanted to come as a pirate."

He laughed. "That would work well for you, too."

She waved her wand at him. "Which is what you are, obviously."

"How did I do?"

Antonia inspected his costume—a white shirt with a scarlet sash, a big gold earring, a plumed hat, breeches, and high boots. Neither his father nor the Regent had been amused by his choice, both leaping to the conclusion that he was throwing his past in the face of the *beau monde.*

They were right.

"You need an eye patch to complement your scar," she said.

He snorted. "Only an idiot would wander around Vauxhall with an eye patch. I'd miss half the thieves out to pick my pocket."

"I can't imagine anyone being stupid enough to try to rob you. But that earring of yours is splendidly barbaric, I must say."

When she went up on tiptoe to inspect the dangling gold hoop, Roman had to resist the impulse to pull her in close.

"It's quite a lovely piece," she said.

"I agree," he said gruffly.

"Where did you get it?"

"I'll tell you another time. Right now, I'd best return you to your friend so he'll stop glaring daggers at me."

"He's actually glaring at me." Antonia held up a finger to indicate that the young man should wait. "There's something I need to say to you before I go back, sir."

"So, this wasn't purely a social visit."

She smiled. "No, you distracted me."

I'd like to distract you more.

He squashed the errant image of Antonia Barnett naked in his arms. Fantasies of embracing naked women were hardly unusual for him, but they normally involved big chested, sexually robust lasses, not slender fairy queens.

"Very well. I am all ears, Miss Barnett," Roman said.

She drew in a breath, as if for courage, causing her breasts to swell up in tempting little mounds over the tightly wrapped bodice. "I wish to apologize for my rude behavior the other night."

"What rude behavior?"

"The bit at the end, when I stammered like an idiot and fled your box?"

He forced himself to stop looking at her bodice. "Yes, that was rather odd."

"That's the word for me. Odd," she said ruefully.

"I meant your behavior was odd. Since you didn't bat an eyelash when your father and I were squaring off, I wasn't sure what had flustered you so badly."

She flapped a hand. "I'm used to Papa's moods. They're harmless."

Barnett was anything but harmless.

"Then what upset you?" he asked.

"You're the Duke of Clarence's son. That threw me off a bit."

"Because I'm a bastard?"

"No, because you're the son of a *prince*. I wasn't expecting that."

"I'm still a bastard."

She waggled a hand. "A royal one."

"That fact doesn't truly mitigate the scandalous circumstances of my birth or the shame that comes with it. I should think you would understand better than anyone."

Her gaze narrowed. "It's really quite rude of you to be so frank about *my* situation. It's supposed to be a secret."

"One of the worst kept in London, I'd wager."

She blew out an exasperated sigh. "True enough. But it does seem unfair in my case. After all, my parents did eventually marry. It's annoying that people make such a fuss, as if I'm somehow hideously marked for life."

As inconvenient as it sometimes was to be the by-blow of a prince, Roman had a standing and degree of privilege denied to most others born out of wedlock. The Duke of Clarence's support had opened doors and provided opportunities he'd been quick to leverage. And with the right sort of wife, he could climb higher still on the rungs of prosperity and power.

Antonia's options, however, were limited.

"You're right," he said softly. "It's not fair at all."

"I don't care that much for my sake, but it's hard on my parents. Papa gets so upset when people say nasty things about me."

"Ergo the dunking."

She let out a reluctant chuckle. "Poor Lord Totten. It wasn't even much of an insult."

Lord Totten could go to perdition, as far as Roman was concerned. "Miss Barnett, there is nothing scandalous about you, except for a certain penchant for wandering off by yourself."

"Everyone has to have a hobby."

"Please tell me you're joking."

She batted that aside. "If you want to know what I think—"

"Not that you won't tell me anyway."

"In my opinion, neither of us is shameful *or* scandalous," she said firmly. "At least not by virtue of the actions of our parents. If people want to gossip and make false assumptions, that's not our fault."

Roman found himself hoping she'd never hear the gossip about his notorious past, much of it true.

"So my father keeps telling me," he said, forcing a lighter tone. "He's determined to see me reformed in the eyes of polite society."

"I didn't know you needed to be reformed." She tilted her head. "Perhaps that's why Papa is averse to a friendship between us. He's wants me to snag a rich, boring aristocrat with no scandal attached to his name."

"Did your father say anything about me, specifically?"

"No. Papa just said I was to steer clear of you."

"And yet here you are."

"Mamma wouldn't mind. She even remarked favorably on your, er, personal assets."

He practically choked. "I'm sure that went down well with your father."

Her golden gaze twinkled. "He wasn't in the room at the time."

When the first strains of a waltz drifted over from the orchestra pavilion, she glanced back at her friend. "Oh, the dancing is starting. I'd better get back to Richard or he'll pitch a fit."

"Are you promised to him for the first waltz?"

"No, but he'll worry if he can't keep an eye on me."

"Has anyone asked you to dance?"

Her tiny sigh, barely audible, made something go tight in his chest.

"Then dance with me, Miss Barnett. I'll keep you safe."

Her lips parted in surprise. "I...I really shouldn't," she stammered.

"Why not?"

"Well, people might not like it."

Meaning her father. Even behind the elaborate mask he could read that she longed to say yes.

He gently wrapped his fingers around her small hand. "Surely the queen of the fairies answers only to herself."

She stared at him for a few seconds longer, then her cheerful, engaging grin slipped free. "I do believe you are right, sir." Still holding his hand, she dipped into a curtsy. "I should be honored."

When he led her to the dancing area, Richard Keane rushed up to them.

"Confound it, Tony," the young man blustered. "What the devil—"

"I'll see you after the dance," she called out as Roman swept her into the first turn.

She danced with a graceful energy, lithe in his arms. Her unabashed enthusiasm was charming, innocent, and entirely infectious. Something awakened in him that Roman hadn't felt in a long time.

Simple, unaffected pleasure.

"Tony?" he said, arching his eyebrows.

"It's dreadful, isn't it?"

"Actually, I think it's rather endearing."

A ladylike snort was her only reply.

They circled through another turn, Roman steering her away from an overly enthusiastic middle-aged couple. A few steps brought them in front of the Regent's supper box, where Roman encountered his father's scowl.

"The Duke is glaring at us," Antonia said.

"As is your friend—along with the lady by his side."

She craned around him to look, not missing a step. "Oh, Richard's mother. She wants me to marry him, so she's probably annoyed that I'm dancing with you, not him."

"And how does young Richard feel about the proposed marriage?"

"He said he'd rather drown himself than marry me."

"What a blockhead."

She sparkled up at him, as if he'd paid her the most extravagant compliment.

"If he doesn't want to marry you," Roman said, "why is he so annoyed?"

"Because he knows Papa would be displeased. Aside from the fact that my father dislikes you— although I'm still not sure why—I'm supposed to be snagging a respectable aristocrat, remember? Not scampering about with you."

"I'm sure my father is thinking exactly the same thing."

"Then since we're both in heaps of trouble, we might as well enjoy it."

He was beginning to think he'd like nothing better than to get into trouble with Antonia Barnett. Still, it would be a huge mistake for both of them.

All too soon, the waltz came to an end. He spun her in one last turn, bringing them to a gentle halt by a stand of walnut trees. Her cheeks were prettily flushed, and her full mouth curved in a joyful smile that seemed to beg him for kisses.

"Thank you, sir. That was utterly wonderful."

She was utterly wonderful—blunt to a fault, but with an innocence and sweetness to her nature that called to him.

That artless innocence was exactly why he needed to sound the retreat.

He stepped back and gave her a formal bow. "You are most welcome, Miss Barnett. And now I should take you back to your friends."

She went still, and a moment later all the pleasure was snuffed from her gaze. "Of course," she said. "You must wish to return to your family."

He nodded, not wanting to say anything that would sound even more dismissive. He was about to take her arm when he felt something round and hard press into his back and knew exactly what it was.

"Don't make a fuss," came the growl from behind him. "Or I'll blow yer stinkin' guts all over the ground."

***

It had all been going so splendidly, especially when Roman pulled her close to his powerful body and spun her into that magical waltz. Even though she hardly knew him, simply being in his arms had filled her with a joy that made her giddy. He was so different from other men. He went head-on for all the tricky bits but treated her with humor and respect. With him, Antonia didn't even feel odd. She felt interesting, and perhaps even desirable.

But when their dance ended, he'd withdrawn, making it clear their budding friendship was at an end. And who could blame him? Despite his illegitimate status, he was the son of a prince. Roman Cantrell was clearly slated for better things than marriage to the socially awkward, slightly scandalous daughter of a trader.

Now, on top of everything else, they were about to be robbed.

She glanced over her shoulder at three men lurking in the shadows under the trees. Their hats were pulled low, and they wore scarves over their chins. The one behind Roman held a gun to his back. Antonia suspected the others were armed as well.

"We're in the middle of the Grove, for Christ's sake," Roman said. "You're really going to rob us here?"

"We ain't in the middle of the Grove, and we ain't gonna rob you," came the answering growl. "Back up, the both of you."

"Let the girl go," Roman said in a tight voice. "Then I'll give you whatever you want."

Their captor let out a low, ugly laugh. "We'll get what we came for, Captain, but you back up now or I'll shoot you both on the spot."

Antonia exchanged a startled glance with Roman. He'd clearly been targeted, but why?

"We'd best do as he wants," she said, worried for him.

Roman quietly cursed before directing a killing glare at the men. "Very well. But if you hurt my companion, I'll throttle you with my bare hands."

When one of the men clamped a hand on Antonia's shoulder and pushed her toward the trees, she dropped her wand in the dirt. Roman let out a snarl at the rough handling, but the men ignored him, hustling them both into the trees, away from the lights and noise of the Grove.

As bad luck would have it, they were heading toward one of the more secluded corners of the Gardens. Unlike the old days, most of Vauxhall was now well lit, precisely to prevent this sort of activity. But there were still a few dark corners where lovers engaged in illicit activity and innocents strolled at their peril. Antonia suspected that their captors had been watching Roman, and waiting for the best moment to take him.

This was no simple robbery.

Roman took her hand. "Don't worry, I'll protect you," he murmured.

He seemed entirely in control and not the least bit worried about the outcome of this unpleasant adventure. Whatever was going to happen, she knew he would do his utmost to protect her.

Antonia's skittering nerves started to settle, allowing her to think clearly.

They tramped in grim silence until they came to the wall that marked the edge of the Gardens.

There were only a few lanterns scattered among the trees, providing but a fitful light. The sounds of the orchestra had faded, as had the noise of the revelers. Only minutes away, hundreds of people ate, danced, and chattered. She and Roman could very well suffer an ugly fate, and no one would be the wiser until too late.

Roman gave her hand a final squeeze before letting go and putting some space between them. He obviously wanted to give himself room to act when he saw an opening.

Do the same.

Antonia inched away from the man guarding her, noting the small pistol he'd pointed directly at her. When Roman turned to face their captors, putting the wall to his back, she followed his lead.

"Gentlemen, perhaps we can now proceed with the robbery," he said. "That way we can all get on with our evening with no harm done."

The leader shook his head. "I told you—this ain't no robbery. But we'll take care of that, once the other bit's done."

That sounded disturbingly ominous.

Roman tilted his head, as if merely curious. "Do you have any idea who I am?"

"Aye. Cantrell, captain of the *Mary Lynn*."

She felt rather then saw Roman freeze, like a predator who'd just realized he was on the wrong end of the hunt.

"I'm also the owner of Cantrell & Sons Shipping," he said. "Which means I'm well able to pay any ransom you want to let the lady go."

"Captain Cantrell is also the son of the Duke of Clarence," she said. "There will be retribution of the highest order if you hurt him."

The other two men shifted uneasily, but the leader remained unmoved. "We know who he is, and we could give a shite."

That was bad, very bad. If the threat of royal vengeance didn't concern them, what would?

"And Griffin Steele is Captain Cantrell's cousin," she added, taking a desperate stab.

"Steele?" said one of the other men. "Bloody hell."

"Antonia, please stop trying to help," Roman said.

"Mr. Steele will be very annoyed to know we've been threatened," she persisted. "And I've heard he's quite bloodthirsty in exacting his revenge." Antonia had no idea if that was true, but she hoped it sounded frightening.

Roman leaned down and murmured in her ear. "You're giving them another reason to murder us on the spot."

While that made no sense, she had to admit she didn't know much about the mental reasoning of the criminal classes.

"We don't give a shite about your threats," snapped their captor.

Antonia made a final effort. "My father is Captain Anthony Barnett. He's rich, and he'll pay you, too."

"Maybe we should take the girl up on it," put in one of the underlings. "This ain't turning out right. He's late."

"Shut your gob," their leader snapped. "We promised him, and I won't go back on my word."

"Care to tell me who *he* is?" Roman asked in a casual tone.

"You'll find out soon enough. Then you'll pay for what you did to our family."

Antonia pressed a hand to her stomach. So this was personal. She couldn't help wondering what Roman had done to make himself a target of such bloodthirsty intent. But she couldn't worry about that now. They had to make their move before Roman's unknown enemy showed himself.

She let out a little shriek and pointed toward the dark woods. "Is that he?"

That her gambit worked didn't say much for the intellect of their captors. When the men peered into the trees—one actually turning around to do so—Antonia reached down and pulled the knife from the leather sleeve strapped to her calf. She quickly spun and sliced at the arm of the man holding Roman at gunpoint. He yelped and jerked up, accidentally discharging his pistol. In an incredible piece of good luck, the ball struck one of the other men, who clapped a hand to his shoulder and stumbled back with a loud groan.

Roman threw himself on the leader, taking him hard to the ground. "Antonia, run," he barked as he grappled with the man.

She would do no such thing, although she took a few steps back and kept a wary eye on the wounded man and his companion, who seemed at a loss what to do. Her well-balanced blade was exceedingly sharp, and she had little doubt she could hit one of them if she threw it, despite her rattled nerves. Fortunately, the two scoundrels appeared to have lost interest in her.

"Come on, Bob," shouted the uninjured man. Holding onto each other, they took off at a stumbling run for the cover of the trees.

The third man, meanwhile, gave a great heave and flung Roman off, then leapt to his feet and took off after the others. Rolling into a crouch, Roman came smoothly upright but made no attempt to pursue their attackers.

"What are you doing?" she exclaimed. "You're letting them escape!"

His ferocious scowl was evident even in the fitful light of the distant lanterns. Grabbing Antonia's elbow, he propelled her toward the path back to the Grove.

"Of course I'm letting them go."

"Why, for heaven's sake?"

"The one I took down had another pistol in his coat. I felt it during our ridiculous wrestling match. I couldn't take the chance he would get it out and shoot one of us."

"Why didn't you pull out *your* pistol and shoot *him*?"

"Because I don't have a bloody pistol on me."

She blinked. "I would have thought you always carried one. My father does."

It sounded like he was grinding his molars. "I am not in the habit of carrying weapons when I attend social occasions. They hardly seem like an appropriate accessory while dancing with pretty girls."

"Not generally, I suppose." Which was unfortunate in this case.

"Speaking of weapons, where did you get that knife?" he asked.

"From under my skirts."

"You carry a blasted knife under your skirts?"

They'd broken free of the trees and were now on one of the lighted paths. Just ahead was the colonnaded walkway, packed with strollers.

Antonia pulled him to a stop and bunched up her hem, showing him the sleeve strapped to her calf. After carefully wiping her blade on some leaves, she slipped the knife back into its holder.

Roman stared at her leg, apparently struck dumb.

"Papa had this made for me a few years ago," she said. "He says that knives are much more dependable than pistols."

"Your father taught you how to throw a knife?" he asked with disbelief.

She nodded. "After someone tried to rob me in Wapping a few years ago, in broad daylight, if you can believe it."

He shook his head, muttering something that was best ignored.

"Anyway, when Papa is not with me, he insists that I carry a blade. I usually strap it to my leg. It's easier to access that way, even if it sometimes put snags in my stockings."

"He should have gotten you a bodyguard, instead."

"He tried, but I put my foot down. Fortunately, Mamma agreed with me that a bodyguard was unnecessary."

He eyed her with a look she couldn't decipher. Antonia felt a blush creep into her cheeks. After all, genteel young ladies generally didn't go about stabbing people, no matter how warranted.

"You are completely mad," he finally said.

His words hurt more than they should, especially since she barely knew him. Still, she felt a connection with him, one she'd never experienced with another man. And for a few minutes, she'd thought Roman had felt the same.

Clearly, she'd been mistaken.

"My madness saved our lives, Captain Cantrell." She started toward the Grove.

He grasped her arm and reeled her back in. "Don't run off."

"Why not?" she asked gruffly. "So you can insult me some more?"

"No, so I can apologize for being an ungrateful thickhead. I'm not used to young ladies rescuing me at knifepoint. It's unnerving, since I'm supposed to do the rescuing."

She'd hurt his pride. "I'm sure you would have done so at the first opportunity."

"Yes, that was my plan," he said dryly.

He must think her a complete hoyden, and she couldn't blame him. Still, it was better than being dead.

"I commend you on keeping your wits," he added. "It was a frightening situation."

"I was a bit rattled but also fairly confident we'd be able to handle them. After all, you *are* a ruthless sea captain, are you not?"

He snorted. "Antonia, allow me to say that you are a decidedly unusual girl."

She sighed. "You mean odd, don't you?"

A funny sort of smile played around the corners of his hard mouth. For a crazed moment, she was tempted to drag his head down and taste his lips.

"I didn't say that," he said in a low, seductive voice as he leaned a fraction closer.

For a glorious moment she thought *he* was going to kiss *her*. The breath caught in her throat as she swayed toward him.

Suddenly, he pulled back. After casting a quick glance behind him, he took her arm and headed for the Grove.

Inside, Antonia felt something deflate. She'd wanted that kiss more than she'd wanted anything in a very long time.

Well, perhaps he was distracted by the fact that someone had just tried to kill them. That was certainly a reasonable and more comforting explanation for his obvious reluctance.

"Do you have any idea who those men were?"

"I do not," he said. "But I will find out."

"Maybe the man they were waiting for is one of your business rivals. Papa always says shipping and trade are very cutthroat."

"I'm sure he's speaking metaphorically. English traders aren't generally in the habit of murdering each other."

"I can ask Papa about it. He might have heard rumors."

Roman pulled her to a stop and clamped his hands on her shoulders. "You are not to say a word to your father, understand?"

"But—"

"Antonia, if he finds out you were at risk because of me, then one English trader *will* murder another. So unless you want to see your father on his way to the gallows for dispatching me, keep your pretty mouth firmly buttoned."

She waved an annoyed hand. "Oh, very well. Although I truly don't think Papa would murder you."

"Let's not test that theory, shall we?"

"Tony, thank God!"

They turned to see Richard dashing toward them, his pharaoh's crown tilted sideways on his head. He shoved a pair of inebriated Vikings out of the way as he pelted up, waving her bedraggled wand.

"Where have you been?" he demanded. "I found your wand lying on the ground and thought you'd been dragged off." His gaze darted over her figure. "You look a mess. One of your wings is twisted."

She craned around, trying to glimpse her back. "Oh, dear. Those wings were quite expensive, too."

Her friend glared at Roman. "What did you do to her, you scoundrel?"

"Captain Cantrell didn't do anything," she said firmly. "In fact, he rescued me after we were accosted by thieves."

Roman cast Richard a sardonic gaze. "It was Miss Barnett who effected our rescue, in point of fact."

"Used your knife, did you?" Richard said. "Good for you, Tony."

"You know she carries a knife strapped to her leg?" Roman said in a disapproving tone.

"And a good thing she does, too. Thought she'd be safe in *your* company, Captain Cantrell. It's the only reason I let her go talk to you."

"Richard, I do not need your permission to talk to Roman...Captain Cantrell," Antonia said. "I don't need your permission to talk to anyone."

Her friend thrust out a stubborn jaw. "It's my job to look out for you when your father isn't here."

"Good job, so far," Roman said with a snort.

"Well, it sounds like you didn't cover yourself in glory either," Richard said hotly. "You should be grateful Tony was there to pull you out of a such a kick up. Huzzah for her."

Roman ignored him. "Miss Barnett, I suggest that you and Mr. Keane return to the Grove immediately. Better yet, go home and try to stay the hell out of trouble."

On that blighting note, he stalked into the woods, quickly vanishing into the night.

CHAPTER THREE

Antonia bounced the baby on her lap, smiling as the little girl chortled with glee.

"You're very good with children," Lady Hunter said with an approving nod. "Most young ladies of the *beau monde* hardly know how to even hold them."

"I suppose they're never given the chance." Antonia carefully extracted a stray lock of her hair from the baby's fist. "Their lives are so regimented, and then they're sent away to school when they're still so young."

"You were not, I take it."

"Papa wouldn't hear of it. He said we'd all been apart for too long, and he had too much time to make up with his daughter." No point in pretending Papa was only her stepfather, since it was clear that Lady Hunter already knew the truth.

"Good for him. I could never abide the practice of separating children from their parents at such an early age. It's barbaric." Her ladyship placed her teacup on the little wrought iron table between them. "And speaking of barbaric, Lisbet is demolishing your coiffure. Let me take her so you can finish your tea."

They were in the lush rose garden behind Lady Hunter's manor house in Camberwell, which served as both her home and her establishment for unfortunate girls and their babies. Her ladyship had sent a gracious invitation to both Mamma and Antonia to discuss her charity work, so they'd made the hour-long drive out to the village to spend the afternoon.

Unfortunately, a little subterfuge had been necessary, since Mamma had insisted they keep their outing a secret.

"Your father will raise a ridiculous fuss, forcing me to put my foot down," Mamma had said. "Whatever his objections might be to Griffin Steele, Sir Dominic and Lady Hunter are above reproach. I wouldn't dream of offending that good woman by refusing her invitation."

"I don't think it's about Griffin Steele," Antonia had replied. "It's Captain Cantrell he objects to."

"Well, that's between your father and the captain. Besides, I very much doubt Cantrell will be there. This is a charitable outing, not a party."

Since Antonia very much wanted to further her acquaintance with Lady Hunter and her family, she found her mother's logic quite compelling. And if she and Mamma were forced to tell a few fibs about where they were going today, well, it was for

Papa's own good. Captain Cantrell wouldn't be anywhere near a charitable establishment. And even if he were, he had no interest in her anyway. He'd made that perfectly clear the other night when he'd dumped her back in Richard's care and stalked off.

Antonia handed over the squirming little tyke.

"I take it you didn't mind not attending a girl's seminary," Chloe said as she handed Lisbet off to the nursemaid who'd just come out to fetch her.

"Lord, no. But I don't think I would have done very well, anyway," Antonia said.

"Nonsense. You're obviously an exceedingly intelligent young woman. Too intelligent for the average girl's seminary, I suspect."

"It wasn't that. I just didn't possess the knack for getting along with most of the other girls. Papa let me go as a day pupil to Miss Barton's school in London for a term." She gave her hostess a rueful smile. "Let us just say I was an abject failure."

Lady Hunter cocked a knowing eyebrow. "The other girls teased you?"

"Rather unmercifully, I'm afraid. I didn't take it very well."

"I had a similar experience. My guardian sent me away to boarding school when I was fifteen. I also had difficulty fitting in."

"I suspect you didn't deliver an uppercut to a schoolmate's jaw, did you?" After suffering one too many insults about her parents, Antonia had finally taken justice into her own hands.

Lady Hunter almost spilled her tea. "No, but in retrospect, I wish I had. Were you asked to leave?"

"Yes, and Papa thought it best I study at home from then on. I'm sure my classmates agreed," Antonia said with a chuckle. "Mamma tutored me in the usual subjects, and Papa also had me down to his offices to learn mathematics, navigation, and bookkeeping."

"That sounds vastly more interesting than going to school."

"I enjoyed it very much. There was always a great deal of activity and something new to learn. And it was particularly exciting whenever one of Papa's ships came into port." Antonia closed her eyes and breathed out a sigh, enjoying the warmth of the sun on her face. "To tell you the truth, I miss it."

"You don't visit your father's offices anymore?"

She opened her eyes to see Lady Hunter studying her with a great deal of sympathy. "He says it's not appropriate for respectable young ladies to be spending time in a business environment. Papa is afraid I'll damage my prospects on the Marriage Mart. As if they don't already know that my father is a trader," she said, flapping a hand.

"I believe your mother's father was a viscount, was he not?"

Antonia refreshed her cup from the dainty Sevres teapot that sat between them. "For most of the *ton*, that's hardly enough to erase the odor of commerce that clings to the Barnett family name."

"I find that most of them are idiots and best ignored."

"I much prefer Nightingale Trading to Mayfair. When one of Papa's ships comes into port, it's like the entire world has arrived at our door." Antonia wrinkled her nose. "But now I'm expected to spend my days on rounds of boring visits with disapproving mothers and sit about at dreary balls with the rest of the unfortunate wallflowers."

Lady Hunter flashed her a wry smile. "When you put it like that, I'm happy I managed to avoid that situation."

"I don't mean to sound ungrateful," Antonia said, "especially since my father simply wants the best for me. But I seem to have a fatal knack for the saying the wrong thing, especially to men. I just wish I had something useful to do with my life instead of waiting for some man to decide he wishes to marry me. Something like you do, Lady Hunter."

"You do have a say in the process, my dear girl."

"Some days I wonder."

Lady Hunter fell silent, her gaze on a fragrant bed of blush pink roses. Antonia surrendered to the beauty of the old-fashioned rose garden and the peace of a country village on a late summer's day. Mamma was still inside with Justine Steele, talking with the residents and spending time with the children. Antonia had little doubt her mother would make an offer of patronage to support the charity's excellent work.

And perhaps Antonia might even be able to volunteer in Camberwell a few days a week. It would be something worthwhile and might help to calm her restless spirit.

Her hostess finally stirred from her reverie. "Have you not met any young men you find interesting?"

One, but he's not all that young, nor is he very interested in me.

"Not really."

"What about Richard Keane? He seems very nice."

"We're more like brother and sister than anything else."

"That will never do," Lady Hunter said with a twinkle. "What about my nephew, Captain Cantrell? He's a very nice man, if a bit intimidating. You seemed to get along quite well that night you met him, until he apparently frightened you off."

Antonia grimaced. "I was flummoxed when he told me that his father was the Duke of Clarence. I acted like a complete ninny."

"I'm sure Roman doesn't think so."

"Actually, he thinks I'm a hoyden."

"Why would he think that?"

"I did speak to the captain at the masked ball the other night, and we sorted out the confusion over his father. But then we had, um, a little contretemps."

Lady Hunter's eyebrows shot up. "You were with Roman when he was held up? My dear, how upsetting for you. I had no idea."

"Yes, it was distressing for both of us. Captain Cantrell, though, was mostly upset that I pulled out my knife and cut one of our captors."

Her ladyship looked taken aback. "That was intrepid of you. Do you always carry a knife?"

"Usually." She sighed. "I know it's not very ladylike."

After a fraught pause, Lady Hunter grinned at her. "I think it's splendid that you defended yourself. In fact, you'd fit right in with the women in our family, I assure you."

"Really?"

"Really, and I'm sure Roman found you both enterprising and delightful."

"We can pretend he did, anyway," Antonia said.

"There's no need to pretend. You can ask him yourself right now."

She followed Lady Hunter's gaze to see Roman striding out the French doors and down to the lawn. Antonia had to resist the impulse to curse and slink behind the nearest bush.

When she got a good look at him, she was glad she hadn't. In the light of day, Roman Cantrell was even more handsome and imposing than he'd been under the glittering lights of Vauxhall. Garbed in a burgundy riding coat, tight-fitting breeches, and shiny black boots, he looked so delicious she wanted to fan herself. And when sunlight glinted off his gold earring, perversely highlighting his rampant masculinity, her heart seemed to trip over itself. If Antonia was the type of girl who fainted, she suspected she'd be on the ground right now.

Of course, since they hadn't parted on the best of terms, a maidenly swoon would likely be wasted on him.

Lady Hunter rose from her wrought-iron seat. "Roman, my dear, what a delightful surprise."

He paused for a fraction too long. "Er, yes. I hope I'm not intruding. I was just passing by Camberwell and thought I'd pop in."

As if one happened by little country villages every day. It appeared that Lady Hunter enjoyed matchmaking, too.

Antonia swallowed a laugh and rose to her feet. "Captain Cantrell, how delightful to see you."

He bowed over her hand. "Yes, it is indeed a charming surprise."

"Just imagine us running into each other like this again. Life certainly can take an odd turn, don't you think?"

"Indeed."

Lady Hunter looked at the watch attached to her sash. "I must go in and check on one of my charges. I'll return shortly. In the meantime, Roman, I expect you to keep Miss Barnett entertained."

"Yes, Aunt."

She gave her nephew a stern look. "Do not frighten her off."

"Don't worry, ma'am," Antonia said. "If he starts acting like a bear, I'll simply pull out my knife and stab him."

Lady Hunter laughed, and with a wave disappeared into the house.

Roman sank into the empty chair. He didn't wait for her to sit first, treating her as he would a male companion. Antonia found she rather liked that. It made them feel like...equals.

"So you told her about our little adventure in Vauxhall, did you?" he said. "I was trying to protect you from gossip."

She shrugged. "I haven't heard any, if that's what you're worried about."

"Only insofar as it hurts you."

"I'm fairly immune to gossip at this point."

"There's gossip and then there's gossip, Antonia."

She had to struggle to hide the thrill that shot through her when he spoke her name in that lovely, deep voice. "I'm not sure I follow."

"While it's unfortunate that people gossip about your ostensibly scandalous parentage, no true blame attaches to you for that."

"No true blame attaches to Mamma or Papa, either," she said in a warning tone.

"Naturally, but the gossip would be of quite a different nature if people found out we'd been gallivanting about in the darker walks of Vauxhall alone."

"Not alone, at least for part of it. And we were trying to save our lives, which hardly counts as gallivanting."

"I'm afraid many in the *ton* will find that a minor detail, easily ignored."

Antonia snorted. "I suppose they would think it better if I had ended up murdered, as long as my reputation remained intact."

He cut her a wry smile. "Yes, they are generally an appalling bunch, but I won't see you harmed on my account."

"I'm grateful, but there's no harm done."

"There might be if you don't take better care of yourself."

She resumed her seat. "I take perfectly good care of myself, my dear sir."

His only reply was an annoying snort.

"Why are you here?" she asked bluntly. "This hardly seems like your sort of outing."

"How straightforward you are, Miss Barnett. I do find it refreshing."

"You know I'm not very polished. Now, please answer the question."

His dark, amused gaze lingered on her face, pulling warmth into her cheeks.

"Perhaps I knew you would be here," he said.

Now it was her turn to scoff.

He leaned forward and rested his forearms on his muscular thighs, loosely clasping his hands. "Don't underestimate your charms, Antonia," he said, giving her a sideways glance.

She told herself to ignore his flattery. "You obviously came because you knew I was going to be here, even though Lady Hunter pretended your appearance was a surprise."

"Caught that, did you?"

"I suspect she's matchmaking."

He jerked upright. "Really?"

She waggled a hand. "I'm fairly certain of it."

"I don't mean to criticize, but aren't young ladies supposed to keep that sort of speculation to themselves?"

"Well, you are the other intended victim. I thought you should know."

He went back to looking sardonic. "You are definitely the most unusual girl I've ever met."

"I believe you've made that point already, sir."

"I don't mind in the least, I assure you. Leaving Aunt Chloe's machinations to the side for the moment, I'm glad for the opportunity to speak with you without irate fathers or annoying pickpockets to interrupt."

"Those weren't just pickpockets, and you know it."

He rolled his lips inward, looking like he didn't want to answer. "You're right," he finally said.

"So that's why you disappeared so precipitously. You were going to look for them."

A hard nod was her answer.

"I take it you didn't find them."

"They were long gone by the time I got back to that part of the Gardens."

"Did they leave any clues?"

He frowned. "Like what?"

"Oh, I don't know. A handkerchief with an initial on it, or one of their pistols—"

"Or a letter with an address conveniently written on the envelope," he interrupted.

"There's no need to be sarcastic. I did help save us, you know."

"I do know. Although I admire your courage, I still find it deeply disturbing that I put you in that situation. You could have been injured, or worse."

"That's why you wanted to see me, isn't it? You wanted to apologize."

When he nodded, she had to swallow her disappointment. Despite his gallant teasing, it was silly to think that he had any interest in her as a woman.

"Thank you, but I'm perfectly fine. And I have no doubt you would have effected my rescue one way or another, regardless of my efforts."

His smile was rueful. "I will comfort myself with that knowledge."

"I certainly hope they leave you alone from now on. Do you have any idea who they were?"

When he shrugged, she rolled her eyes. "Let me guess—one of your business rivals."

"Probably."

"Do all your competitors wish to murder you?" she asked politely.

That prompted a grin. "Your father certainly does."

"My father has many business rivals, and he's generally quite friendly with them. The way he reacted to you…" She shook her head. "Well, it's not like him."

While Papa could be ruthless when it came to business, he was also a fair and honest man with a good heart.

"He's not my favorite person, either," he said dryly.

"I wish you would tell me why. It's annoying the way you both dance around the question."

"Ah, so you talked to him about me. What did he say?"

"He refused to talk about you."

Roman laughed.

"Captain Cantrell," she started in an irritated tone.

"Your father and I have been in direct competition on a number of important contracts. He does not appreciate that Cantrell & Sons was able to outbid him more than once. Of course, competition works both ways. I was just about to sign a lucrative order with the Kingdom of Naples when your esteemed papa stole it right out from under my nose." He let out a disgusted snort. "It made me look like a complete idiot."

No wonder Roman had been so aggressive with her father the other night. Papa had clearly wounded his masculine pride.

"Stole?" she said politely.

"It's how we describe such things. He very adroitly underbid me at the last moment."

"Papa is a very good businessman, but nothing you've said has explained his hostility."

"Antonia, why are you so interested in this?"

She willed herself not to blush under his intent gaze. "My mother would be very annoyed if Papa murdered you. And we both would be very annoyed if you murdered my father. So tell me what the problem is, and I'll see if I can somehow help."

"I suspect it has to do with the fact that I was a privateer during the war," he said reluctantly.

"You mean you held a letter of marque? So did many merchants during the war, including my father."

"No, I was a privateer. That's not the same thing as an armed merchantman. You do know the difference, do you not?"

She scowled at him. "I am Anthony Barnett's daughter. Of course I know."

"Then you also know that privateering vessels are bigger, faster, and armed to the teeth. For the most part, they are made to attack enemy commerce. Vessels like those of Nightingale Trading are mostly armed for defensive purposes and still focus on trade. If an opportunity to seize an enemy prize presents itself..."

"They take it."

"Yes," he said. "But in smaller numbers than privateers."

"But both you and Papa hold letters of marque. They empowered you to act on behalf of the Crown, did they not?"

He nodded.

"Then what am I missing?" she asked.

Roman stared into the distance, although the only thing the distances displayed were clipped shrubbery and more rosebushes.

"There are those who believe privateers are little better than pirates."

"Like my father?"

He shrugged. "He's rather a high stickler."

Papa wasn't, but she let the point go. "And are you a pirate, Captain Cantrell?"

"Of course not."

"No, you're the son of a royal duke. As far as I can tell, neither your father nor your uncles are pirates, either."

"No, just rascals and reprobates."

"That's hardly your fault, either." She exhaled an exasperated sigh. "It hardly seems fair of Papa to hold your service to England against you when he did something similar."

"Things tended to get a bit bloodier on privateering vessels. It wasn't always pleasant."

"From what I understand, war never is," she said. "I still don't think my father should hold it against you."

"He might not agree."

"Sir—"

"He's just trying to protect you, Miss Barnett," he said firmly. "I don't blame him."

She much preferred it when he called her Antonia. Roman had obviously decided to retreat into formality again.

"You mean he's over-protecting me." She studied him for a moment, and then decided to risk it. "Actually, I suspect Papa's behaving so badly because he fears I've developed feelings for you."

Roman looked as stunned as if she'd slapped him.

"And have you developed such feelings?"

Antonia pressed a modest hand to her chest. "As if I would ever be so bold as to reveal my feelings for *any* gentlemen."

The slow smile that parted his lips was both genuine and warm. It made her toes curl with pleasure.

"I've noticed that you're a pattern card of modest behavior," he teased.

"As are you, my dear sir."

"I do try. Ask anyone."

She had to laugh but quickly sobered. "Truly, sir, I am sorry my father is so frosty with you. I'm sure if he had the chance to know you, things would be different."

"And do you think you know me, Antonia?" he asked in a tone that muddled her insides.

"I think so," she whispered.

He bridged the gap between them, coming close. "Could you be more specific?"

His dark gaze roamed over her face, seeming to linger on her mouth.

I think I want you to kiss me.

No, she *knew* she wanted to kiss him. From the look in his eyes, Roman wanted the same thing. He lowered his head, only inches from her lips.

"What the hell is going on out here?" roared a voice from the terrace.

Antonia almost fell over, but Roman quickly rose, moving in front of her chair as if to shield her.

Papa.

She stood and stepped around her misguided protector.

"Antonia," Roman started.

"Trust me, you'll just make things worse."

She pinned on a smile, composing herself while her father charged across the lawn. Mamma and Lady Hunter scampered in his wake, unable to keep up with his ground-eating strides.

"Good afternoon, Papa," she said as he stormed up. "I didn't realize you'd be joining us this afternoon."

"Clearly not, since you and your mother lied about where you were going."

"No, I don't believe we did." Not unless one counted lies of omission.

Her father stabbed a finger at Roman. "And, you. What the hell are you doing with my daughter?"

"I should think it obvious," Roman drawled. "I was ravishing her in the middle of my aunt's rose garden, in broad daylight."

"Not helping," she said, glaring over her shoulder at him.

While Roman gave a casual shrug, she read tension in the set of his broad shoulders.

Her father growled and tried to go around her. She slapped a restraining hand on his chest. "He's just baiting you, Papa."

"Anthony, stop it this instant," said Mamma as she puffed up. "There is no reason to cause a scene."

"Indeed not," added Lady Hunter. "I had my eye on your daughter and my nephew the entire time."

"Then why the devil was he about to kiss her?" Papa barked.

Antonia adopted an expression of wounded innocence. "Papa, as if I would ever behave in so ramshackle a fashion. How could you think that?"

"I know what I saw," her father replied.

"I'm not sure how," Mamma said. "You charged out before you even got a good look at them." She cast Lady Hunter an apologetic glance. "Do accept my apology on my husband's behalf, my lady. I'm mortified."

"As am I," Antonia swiftly added. "It's terribly embarrassing."

"Are you two really going to turn this around on me?" Papa asked.

"Apparently so," Roman said.

Antonia was tempted to drive her heel into his shin. At this point, she wanted nothing more than to give both Roman and her father a good whack.

"It's very bright out here in the garden, Captain Barnett," Lady Hunter calmly interceded. "Your vision was no doubt a bit dazzled when you stepped onto the terrace. Roman would never act inappropriately, I assure you."

Papa scoffed. "Are you sure about that? Because I am not."

"Papa, you're embarrassing us," Antonia said.

"It's all right, Miss Barnett," Roman said. "I'm quite capable of defending myself."

"Of course you are, my dear," Lady Hunter said. "But you've done nothing wrong."

"That's a matter of opinion," Papa said. "What I know for certain, however, is that I don't want you anywhere near my daughter, Cantrell."

"I suppose you don't think I'm good enough for her," Roman said.

"You're not."

Lady Hunter's gaze narrowed with irritation, and Mamma let out an aggrieved sigh.

Antonia decided she'd had enough, too. "Papa, why are you being so difficult? This is ridiculous."

"Perhaps you should ask Cantrell. I'm sure he'd be happy to tell you why I find him so objectionable."

When Roman cursed under his breath, Lady Hunter intervened again.

"There is nothing to tell, Captain Barnett," her ladyship said in an austere voice. "Nothing."

Her father stared at Lady Hunter, clearly startled by her tone. She stared right back at him, as if daring him to raise more objections.

"Papa, it might be wise to remember that our hostess is also Griffin Steele's mother," Antonia said, trying another tack.

"I'm not afraid of Steele, Antonia. Or of Cantrell."

"Oh, for God's sake," Mamma said, exasperated. "Lady Hunter, please forgive us, but I think it's best we make our farewells. Come along, Anthony." She gave a hard yank on her husband's sleeve.

He threw one last angry look at Roman, then allowed his wife to tug him away.

"I'm so sorry," Antonia said miserably. "I don't know what's gotten into him."

"It's not your fault, my dear," said Lady Hunter, patting her shoulder. "Your papa is clearly not himself."

"You'd better go, Miss Barnett," Roman said. "If your father comes back, I cannot answer for the consequences."

She took in his grim expression, then nodded and hurried after her parents.

CHAPTER FOUR

Roman shifted on the small padded chair as he swept his gaze around the dark tent. It was already packed, with only the center ring ablaze with torchlight and free of the jostling crowd. The pugilistic bout between the two combatants, prizefighters nicknamed Emperor and King, was a massive draw. The fact that it was thoroughly illegal hadn't stopped droves of Londoners from attending, including a smattering of females.

It was just the sort of madcap adventure Antonia Barnett was likely to favor, so he breathed a sigh of relief that she wasn't there. Of course, after that humiliating scene in Camberwell, she probably hoped to never cross paths with him again.

"You're as nervous as a cabin boy in his first storm," said the Duke of Clarence in a humorous tone. "Everything will be fine."

Roman looked askance at his father. "We're attending an illegal bout, sir. It's attracted every pickpocket and bounder in London, along with some of the Whitechapel and Covent Garden gangs. I cannot imagine what the Regent was thinking when he decided to grace this little event."

"He was thinking it would be a jolly good time and a splendid opportunity for a wager. Your uncle and I stand to make a tidy sum betting on Gunnery's man. None of his chaps ever lose."

Godrick Gunnery, a former champion himself, was coaching the talented young fighter nicknamed Emperor. Gunnery's presence was a substantial draw, as was that of Gentleman Jackson to officiate the fight. At least with Jackson in charge, the match should be fair.

"True, but since the Duke of Vauxhall's gang is running the wagers, I have a feeling your chances are considerably diminished. In fact, I suspect highway robbery is the most likely outcome."

The crime lord, waggishly named for so effectively claiming Vauxhall Gardens as his territory, was a dangerous sort. With him in the mix, there was little doubt that some criminal scheme was afoot.

His father scoffed. "Not with all these Bow Street Runners mucking about the place. Plus, Devonshire's men are keeping an eye on things. There will be no cheating or stealing, I assure you."

The Runners were out in force. But as far as Roman could tell, they were still outmanned by Vauxhall's gang and other disreputable sorts. Everything he'd ever heard suggested Vauxhall would leave nothing to chance if he could make a profit.

With so many wealthy men here tonight, there was a great deal of profit to be made—or stolen. Roman could feel trouble prickling along the back of his neck. It was the way he always felt when a storm approached just over the horizon, even when a breeze barely stirred.

"I've never met the infamous Duke of Vauxhall," Roman said. "Is he in the tent?"

"Saw him awhile ago," Clarence said, "talking to Devonshire. He wanted to see the ring, I take it."

"Bloody hell," Roman muttered.

The Duke of Devonshire had agreed to sponsor the fight and put up a purse that included a spectacular diamond and gold ring for the winner. The fact that Vauxhall was sniffing around it was not a good sign.

In the last few minutes, more people had crammed into the tent, and the heavy air was beginning to reek of sweat and alcohol. Vauxhall's underlings squeezed through the crowd, taking bets and likely picking pockets. The only empty space was right up by the ring, where several ornate padded chairs stood empty awaiting the arrival of the Regent and his retinue. The boisterous crowd was growing restless, since the fight had been due to start some minutes ago. The organizers clearly didn't wish the Regent's arrival to interrupt the fight, but they might not have a choice.

Roman spied a stealthy hand inch toward the back of his father's coat.

He grabbed it and pulled its owner upright. A frightened boy, no more than ten, stared back at him. Halfway into his cups, Roman's father made a large and inviting target for one of Vauxhall's cubs.

"I didn't mean nothin' by it, mister," yelped the boy, trying to struggle free. "Honest."

"Oh, really?" Roman said, holding him in a firm grip.

Clarence twisted around. "Were you trying to pick my pocket, you blasted rascal? I'll have you transported for trying to steal from a member of the royal family."

Under his layer of dirt, the boy bleached as white as bone.

When Clarence started to wave for a constable, Roman shook his head. "No need for that, sir. The lad was just trying to get closer to see. Isn't that right?"

"Y…yes, your worship."

Roman extracted a half crown from his pocket and gave it to the boy. "Run along now, before you get into trouble."

The youngster cast him a grateful look before slipping back away.

Clarence snorted. "He wasn't trying to get closer, was he?"

"Of course he wasn't."

"Gone soft in your old age, lad?"

"Hardly, but the prisons are crowded enough, as are the transport ships. They don't need more children filling them up."

Roman might have found himself with a similarly desperate life, since Grandfather Cantrell had intended to place him in an orphanage shortly after his birth. If he'd even survived past infancy, he'd probably have ended up on the streets or in a gang, like the cubs roaming the Gardens tonight. Only the Duke of Clarence's intervention had saved him from that fate. Not only had his father provided financial support, he'd made it clear he would take it poorly if his son was not raised in a manner befitting his heritage.

Grandfather Cantrell had eventually accepted Roman for his own sake, and they'd grown close. But he owed his father a debt he could never repay. Clarence knew it, too, which was why he was now so cheerfully trying to manage his son's life.

"Let us not think on dreary subjects like prisons tonight," said Clarence. "You need to relax and enjoy yourself, my boy. The war is finally over."

"I'll try, sir." Not that Roman could ever entirely leave war behind. The memories lurked too near the surface.

"How goes your search on the Marriage Mart?" his father said. "Any promising fillies on the horizon?"

"That is hardly a topic conducive to my relaxation."

Clarence guffawed. "Still having trouble, eh? It's that blasted reputation of yours. Scares the poor chits silly. Plus that damned scar." He shook his head. "Always thought the ladies found scars to be romantic."

"Apparently not mine." Though Antonia didn't seem to mind his scar—or his reputation—at all.

"Not to worry," Clarence said. "I think I've found just the right girl for you."

That sounded alarming. "Who?"

"Lady Serena Tidmore. She's the daughter of an earl and wealthy to boot. Her father's a splendid chap. If I drop a word in his ear, I'm sure he'll be happy to smooth the way."

"Please do not," Roman said. "Unless you wish me committed to Bedlam."

"Met the girl, have you?"

"I have. She's appallingly rigid and judgmental. And I doubt she'd want anything to do with me, given my background."

"She would if her father and I encouraged the match."

"He probably would, because she's already halfway on the shelf."

"Makes no sense, if you ask me. She's a pretty gel with a good dowry."

"She's a mean-spirited gossip, and you know it."

Clarence sighed. "Well, at least she won't be intimidated by you. In fact, I think she's just the woman to keep you in line."

"With respect, sir, I don't wish to be kept in line."

His father adopted a comically woeful expression. "Is it so wrong to wish for you to be happily settled in London, like the rest of my children?"

"You just want me around so you can borrow money," Roman said bluntly.

"Dear boy, I have your cousin Griffin for that. But I'm quite serious when I say you *do* have family, and I don't mean Griffin or the rest of your scapegrace cousins. My children by Mrs. Jordan would be happy to get to know you better. They've told me so any number of times."

Although Roman had met some of his half-siblings, he maintained his distance. They all seemed pleasant enough, but it felt disloyal to his mother's memory to establish a stronger connection with them. Clarence had been devoted to Mrs. Jordan, whereas he'd shown no interest in Roman's mother after their brief affair concluded.

"That is kind of them," Roman said politely.

His father snorted. "I know what that means. My boy, it's time to settle down, spend time with your family, and find a nice little wife. Who knows? The Regent might even give you a title to thank you for your services."

"I don't need—"

His father elbowed him in the ribs. "There's that scoundrel Vauxhall, talking to Devonshire. Looks like they're not going to wait for the Regent, after all."

Roman glanced at Devonshire, who was talking to a surprisingly elegant, slight-looking man.

Except...

"Are you sure that's Vauxhall?" he asked.

His father shot him a frown. "I may be getting old and fat—although not as fat as my brother—but my eyesight is fine. That's the bloody fellow right across from us, in the black coat."

That the Duke of Vauxhall was a woman was stunningly obvious—at least to Roman. He could see it in her slender shoulders and the delicate lines of her face. While her disguise was a masterful one, he couldn't believe she managed to get away with it all these years.

But people generally saw only what they wanted to see, or what they assumed was the truth. His own life had taught him that lesson.

"That is quite a surprise," Roman said.

His father peered at him. "What is?"

"The Duke of Vauxhall is—"

The words died on his lips as he stared in disbelief. It would appear there was another woman prancing about the Gardens dressed as a man—or a boy, more accurately.

"Forgive me, sir," he said as he shot to his feet. "I'll be right back."

"Roman, where are you going?" Clarence exclaimed. "The Regent will be arriving any moment."

"I see someone I must talk to."

"And it can't wait?"

"It cannot."

He grimly shoved his way past a pair of cupshot rakes and headed for the other side of the tent. One of these days, the blasted girl was going to get herself killed. That is, if Roman didn't throttle her first.

***

Antonia tried to peer over the shoulder of the man in front of her. She and Richard were barely ten feet from the boxing ring, but they might as well have been ten miles away. The tent was packed shoulder to shoulder, with more pouring in.

Clearly, half the population of the city wanted to attend the Battle of the Century, as the organizers had deemed the event. But the chances of Antonia actually seeing the fight were diminishing with every passing second. She was beginning to feel rather lightheaded from an atmosphere thick with the odors of sweat, cologne, and liquor. If the bout didn't begin soon, she might cry uncle and ask Richard to take her home.

She could try to get herself safely home if Richard wanted to stay. No one would look twice at her, dressed in breeches and a short jacket and with her hair pinned up under a slouchy hat. But since they were deep in the darkest parts of the Gardens, Antonia had no desire to encounter the disreputable characters lurking about without Richard by her side, disguise or not.

Nor was she as young or as skinny as she used to be. It had been some months since she'd last ventured out dressed as young Tony, and it would appear she'd gained weight—mostly in the bosom and in her bottom, which was tremendously inconvenient. It hadn't been easy to secure a boy's clothing in the first place, and it would be even harder next time around.

Tonight was beginning to feel like trouble. A quiet voice seemed to whisper in her ear, telling her a threatening storm scudded in her direction.

"Bloody hell." Richard scowled at the large man who'd just squeezed in front of them. "You stepped on my foot, you blighter. And you're blocking my view."

The man glanced over his shoulder. "Bugger you, you little shite."

When Richard started to bristle, Antonia grabbed his sleeve. "Leave him alone," she murmured. "We'll get trampled if you start a fight. Besides, he's twice your size."

"We're getting trampled anyway," Richard grumbled. "That imbecile just about crushed my foot."

"As I just mentioned, he's twice your size."

"Oh, very well," Richard said. "But I'm sure I could take him, if I had to."

She bit back a smile. "True, but you'd probably get arrested. Just think what our parents would say if they found out."

"Lord, they'd murder us."

"Especially you. My father would very likely hold you responsible."

Richard grinned. "He knows this sort of escapade would never be my idea. I just tag along to make sure you stay out of trouble."

"Balderdash. You wanted to come tonight as much as I did."

"I wouldn't have bothered if I'd known it would be such a crush. Can't see a blasted thing."

"We could try getting closer to the front. I'll wriggle through first and then you can follow me."

Richard shook his head. "Best to hang back here since half of London is present. Can't take a chance on getting recognized."

"It's so dark in here, no one would be able to tell me from Adam."

He cast a dubious gaze over her figure. "Don't know about that. You're more recognizable than you were a few years ago when we started sneaking out."

"I'm beginning to think getting recognized wouldn't be the worst thing that could happen to me."

He gaped at her. "Did someone drop you on your head? Just think of the scandal if people found out you were…you know."

"That I'm a girl running about in boy's clothing?"

"Hush, you booby. If someone hears us, you'll be ruined."

"That would mean Papa would have to give up his annoying efforts to marry me off to a wealthy aristocrat—which we both know is never going to happen."

Especially since Roman Cantrell had sailed into her life.

Not that the good captain would wish to have anything to do with her after that hideous scene in Camberwell the other day. Antonia had asked her father point-blank why he hated Roman, but he'd gone as tight-lipped as an oyster. Subsequent attempts to broach the subject had resulted in a stern order to stay far away from Roman Cantrell.

It appeared her odd but lovely friendship with Roman was over, a thought so depressing she'd told herself repeatedly that it mattered not a whit. Sadly, her bracing self-lectures had failed to do the trick.

"Trying to ruin yourself is a ridiculous plan," Richard said.

"It's not really a plan, per se. It just occurred to me."

"Well, I'll have none of it. In fact, we're leaving right now."

She stopped him when he tried to grab her arm. "We've gone through a great deal of trouble to get here tonight, including sneaking out of our houses. And I know how much you want to see this fight."

"Tony—"

"I promise I'll be as good as gold. It would be silly to come all this way and then miss the main event."

Richard cast a longing glance toward the ring. "Looks like they're about to get started. I suppose we could stay for a round or two and then sneak out when no one is looking."

"Then why don't we try to move closer? It's bound to get more crowded once Prinny arrives, and I can't see a thing from back here."

"You're right. Clarence arrived about a half hour ago, so the Regent is bound to show soon."

Antonia was about to wriggle through a small gap in front of her, but she jerked back. "Clarence is here? Was anyone with him?"

"Yes, Captain Cantrell." He grimaced. "Oh, blast. Do you think he'll recognize you? Maybe we'd better leave after all."

She tried for a casual shrug. "Cantrell barely knows me. Besides, I'm sure his attention will be on the fight."

"I don't know, Tony—"

"Stop fussing and come along."

Flattening her arms across her chest, she slid between two men blocking their way. Richard swore but followed, apologizing to those who protested when she elbowed them aside or trod on booted toes. They wriggled their way closer, to just behind the ringside corner where Gunnery was deep in conversation with Gentleman Jackson.

Antonia's heart pounded like a hammer against her ribs—not from exertion, but from the fact that she was now within hailing distance of Roman. She could no longer deny her hopeless infatuation with him. She simply *had* to see him again and know he was all right.

Why wouldn't he be, you nitwit?

He hadn't seemed all right in Camberwell after her father had insulted him. For a few moments, Roman had looked truly pained, even haunted, and it had made her heart ache. Whatever troubled him, it must be bad.

That it was also the root of her father's hostility was abundantly clear.

Antonia shaded her eyes against the flare of the torches around the ring, blinking to adjust her vision. When it cleared, she found herself looking straight at Roman, not more than fifteen feet away. He was gazing back at her with a stunned expression that suggested her disguise had catastrophically failed.

His expression swiftly transformed into one of outrage. When he jumped up from his chair, her heart climbed into her throat.

She grabbed Richard's arm. "We've got to get out of here."

"But the fighters are taking their places. See, Jackson is making the introductions."

The crowd started to cheer as Gentleman Jackson introduced the combatants with flourishing language.

Antonia had to shout in Richard's ear to be heard over the din. "Captain Cantrell recognized me."

Startled, Richard glanced across the ring. "Uh, oh, he's headed this way, too. And he looks cross as crabs."

"No, he looks ready to throttle me. Let's go."

As she pulled Richard back the way they came, she spared a glance over her shoulder. Roman was forging toward them with a grim determination that said she needed to be long gone before he reached her.

When Jackson called the fight to begin, the crowd surged closer, pushing Antonia back toward the ring and forcing her to let go of Richard. He grabbed for her but stumbled and was shoved further away. It took only a moment for him to be swallowed up in the heaving throng.

Clamping down on a surge of panic, Antonia made herself as small as she could. For a desperate moment she found herself squeezed between two very drunk men and almost prayed that Roman would find her. But then she remembered what was likely to happen if he did. Wriggling like a fish on a hook, she managed to pop free a moment later.

Finally, she saw the exit and headed for it. She'd almost reached it when a man shot his arms out in response to something happening in the ring and whacked her cap to the ground, sending her hair half tumbling from its pins.

"Sorry, lad." Then the man did a double take and gave her a delighted grin. "Well, what have we here?"

"You have nothing." Antonia snatched up her cap and shoved it back on her head. "Good night to you, sir."

He snaked out a hand and halted her backward shuffle toward the exit. "Oh, don't leave now, my pretty."

The man yanked her close. His clothes were expensive and smelled of bay rum, and she had the vague sense she'd met him before.

Unfortunately, he was also strong, easily preventing her from pulling her knife from her boot—not that she wished to stab him unless absolutely necessary, since that would cause an unholy commotion.

"Unhand me, sir," she ordered.

He squeezed her arm so hard she had to bite back a curse. "I swear I know you."

"You don't."

When he reached for her cap, Antonia kicked him in the shin, solidly connecting.

He yelped. "That hurt, you stupid bitch."

A large hand suddenly came down on his shoulder. "This will hurt even more," Roman said from behind them.

He knocked the man's hand from Antonia's arm, then spun him around and delivered a crushing blow to his chin. The fellow dropped to the ground like he'd been shot.

Antonia was still gaping at him when Roman all but lifted her off her feet. "Come on," he said tersely, propelling her toward the exit.

He used his shoulders and elbows to forge their way through the crowd, like Moses parting the Red Sea. The few who tried to protest took one look at his face and quickly shrank back.

Roman Cantrell was the most awe-inspiring man Antonia had ever met.

He was also a clearly furious man. She started planning how she could slip away before he delivered a thundering scold.

"Don't even think about it," he growled in her ear.

She adopted a wounded expression. "What?"

"Getting away from me. You can run as fast as you can, and I'll still track you down."

That actually sounded rather like fun.

After a few more good shoves, they broke free. Roman hauled her past the crowd gathered around the entrance and onto one of the smaller walks leading to the perimeter of the Gardens. She was all but forced to jog to keep up with his long strides.

"Would you please stop?" she finally spluttered. "My blasted cap is falling off."

He reluctantly ground to a halt. "All right, but hurry."

He half-turned away, both shielding her and keeping on eye on the crowds milling about the tent. His clenched jaw looked hard enough to crack walnuts.

"I don't suppose you saw my friend Richard, did you?" Antonia asked as she shoved her hair under the cap.

He shot her an amazed look. "No, Miss Barnett, I was too occupied with saving your pretty arse from certain disaster."

She tried a placating smile. "I'm happy you came along when you did. That gentleman was very persistent. So, my grateful thanks, my dear sir."

His expression suggested she was a lunatic.

"What?" she asked defensively.

"For the first time in my life, I have sympathy for your father. I don't know how he puts up with you."

That hurt, although she refused to show it. "Since you find my company so distressing, I'll bid you goodnight."

When she tried to march past him, he reeled her back. "Where are you going?"

"To find Richard, of course. He's no doubt waiting for me outside the tent."

Roman shook his head. "He's probably long gone by now."

"Richard would never abandon me. He is a true friend."

"A true friend? He's an utter imbecile." He ran a disapproving gaze over her outfit. "I take it this isn't the first time you've gone prancing about in boys' clothing. You look ridiculous, by the way. I don't know how you expected to get away with this."

She resisted the urge to smack him. "You're the first person to see through my disguise in three years, so you're dead wrong. And I don't prance."

His mouth sagged open. "You've been doing this for three years? You *are* insane."

"I am perfectly sane. Now get out of my way."

He let her push past but he was right on her heels. She threw him back a glare. "Are you coming to help find Richard or just making a pest of yourself?"

"I'm escorting you home. We have to go back this way to get to the boat entrance to the Gardens."

"I don't need—"

Suddenly, they heard shouting ahead of them. Men began streaming out of the tent, running in all directions. The lamps in the tree branches started snuffing out one by one, plunging the Gardens into greater gloom.

"Good God," Roman muttered.

"What's happening?"

He began hauling her further into the darkness. "I don't know, but it can't be good. Those were Bow Street Runners who came bursting out."

She glanced around as he hustled her from the commotion. All through the woods, lanterns were going out like fireflies winking off.

"Who's doing that?"

"People who are up to no good."

A few moments later, he practically yanked her off her feet.

"What in God's name—"

"Hush," he whispered, pulling her behind an oak.

Someone flashed by on the path, slim and sure-footed, before disappearing into the night. A few seconds later, two men barreled after him.

"Those two looked like Runners," she murmured.

"In pursuit of some blackguard, no doubt. We've got to get out of here without being seen."

"Why? We didn't do anything wrong," she said as he pulled her deeper into the cover of the trees.

"No, but someone did, and I don't want you to get caught up in it. You can't be discovered."

"I'm not sure it matters anymore," she muttered.

The entire evening was a complete disaster, anyway.

Except that she was with Roman. Antonia knew he would do anything to protect her, and that knowledge made her insides go soft and muddled. Almost unconsciously, she squeezed his fingers and brushed up closer to his protective warmth.

"Are you all right, Antonia?" he asked gruffly. "You were all but trampled in that blasted tent."

"It was rather crowded, but—"

The ground seemed to collapse underneath her. Roman lifted her right off her feet and scrambled back.

"What was that?" she gasped.

"A trap for some hapless Runner, I expect. Someone dug a pit and covered it up. I don't know what the hell is going on tonight, but it's dangerous. We need to lay low for a bit until things calm down."

Antonia wriggled her toes. Roman's brawny arm encircled her waist, holding her tight in the air. She could feel his impressive strength, and every hard muscle pressed against her back and rear end. That had her heart fluttering like a moth, but not from fear. In fact, she had to repress the instinct to nestle closer, increasing the contact.

Instead, she tapped his arm. "Then you should put me down so we could find someplace safe to hide."

He carefully lowered her to the ground. "I don't suppose you know of any bolt holes close by, do you?"

"As a matter of fact, I do." There were few parts of Vauxhall Gardens that she and Richard hadn't thoroughly explored.

"Why am I not surprised?" he said.

"There's an abandoned grotto by the far wall. Just past that lamp."

A forlorn lantern hung from a nearby tree, beaming a fitful light on what looked like a tumbledown heap of rocks. Antonia led him into the grotto, empty but for an old stone bench and some dried-up leaves that crackled under their boots.

Sinking down onto the bench, she tugged off her cap and let the air cool her flushed skin. Her still irate companion remained standing, his scowl indicating a scold was imminent.

"How many times have you visited this place?" he asked, glancing around.

"A few," she hedged.

"With Richard?"

She nodded, which seemed to annoy him even more.

"And what, exactly, did you and Richard do while sojourning in this charming spot?"

"What do you think we did? We sat on this bench."

"Why don't I believe you?"

Antonia tried not to wince. The first—and last—time she'd ever drunk gin had been here, and she'd promptly gotten sick behind the grotto. That, however, was a much too embarrassing story to share.

"You don't have to believe anything. But I'm telling you that nothing happened. Ever," she added with heavy emphasis.

"Good, because those sorts of escapades are exactly what leads to monumental trouble for young ladies," he said.

She gave a derisive snort. "As if any man would want to dally with me in a dirty old grotto." Although she rather hoped Roman might give it a try.

"You'd be surprised."

"Yes, I would. And if we're going to be here for a while, please cease glaring at me, and sit down. I'm getting a crick looking up at you."

He muttered a few salty oaths then eased down to the bench, careful to stay as far from her as he could. Obviously, Roman didn't wish to dally with her, either. Her record for alienating men remained unbroken.

While he silently fumed beside her, Antonia tried to convince herself it didn't matter. Finally, she decided they'd waited long enough. "This has been a very exciting evening, Captain Cantrell, but I think it's now safe to leave. The commotion appears to have died down."

His head had been canted toward the entrance of the grotto until her words brought him around to face her. "Good God, do you really think this disaster of an evening was exciting?"

"Yes, until you ruined it with your grumpy mood."

"Now you're just being ridiculous."

Her temper finally broke free.
"No, *you're* being ridiculous. If you hadn't come changing across the tent at me, Richard and I would have been able to stay and watch the fight. I'm quite annoyed that you made us miss such an historic event."

She jumped up, intending to stalk past him, but his hand whipped out and clamped around her wrist. The next thing Antonia knew, she was sprawled on his lap, gaping up at his handsome, irate features.

"You want excitement, Miss Barnett?" he said in a tone that made her shiver. "Then I'll be happy to give it to you."

A moment later, his mouth descended to hers in a devastating kiss that swept over her like a raging tide.

CHAPTER FIVE

Antonia Barnett tasted like sunshine, everything wonderful and pure of heart. Roman's heart was far from pure, and he desired her with a need that swamped rational thought. Unfortunately, the poor girl was all but frozen in his embrace, likely from shock.

When he started to pull back, Antonia grabbed his cravat and yanked his head down. She deepened the kiss, tasting him with an eagerness that matched his own. When she mashed closer still, their teeth clinked together.

"Oh, blast," she muttered when he started to laugh. "That was awkward, wasn't it?"

He settled her more securely on his lap, relishing the feel of her curved bottom. Roman wondered if she was wearing smalls under her tight fitting breeches, resisting the urge to explore.

"You're doing fine," he said, nuzzling her kitten-soft cheek. "But there's no need to rush."

Her pretty mouth pursed with doubt. "It is getting rather late, and I'm worried about Richard. I still think we should try to find him."

As well, the longer they lingered the greater the chance of discovery, though Roman didn't care. All he cared about was kissing Antonia again. "Richard can take care of himself."

She let out a breathy sigh and melted against him as he kissed along her delicate jawline. "I suppose so. After all, he knows the Gardens as well as I do."

Roman paused. "How often do you engage in these little outings?"

She gave him a cheeky grin. "You don't want to know. Now, could you please resume what you were doing?"

"You're outrageous," he said before pressing a kiss to her luscious lips.

"You don't truly mind though, do you?" she whispered a moment later.

"I haven't decided yet."

Then he swooped in to ravish her mouth, their tongues swirling with delicious heat. Antonia plastered herself against him, as if she wanted to reach straight to his heart. Roman wanted to be deep inside her, with a passion that sent fire rocketing through his veins. He cradled her as they indulged in long, luxurious kisses, her body turning soft and pliant in his arms.

When she shifted against him, pressing down on his surging cock, he could resist temptation no longer. He slipped a hand under her jacket to cup her lovely breast. The nipple, already pulled into a tight point, poked against the linen of her shirt. Roman thumbed it, smiling against her lips when she jolted against him.

"Too much?"

She took a moment to answer. "Not enough."

When she nipped his lower lip, he went hard as stone. He fumbled with the fall of her breeches, all but ripping the buttons off in his haste. Antonia squirmed impatiently, her fingers tunneling through his hair as she responded with an innocent eagerness that drove him wild.

When he finally got his hand inside her breeches, she felt like heaven, soft and warm, with silky hair tickling his palm.

Antonia jerked back to stare at him. Even in the flickering light of the torch outside the grotto, he could see the flush on her cheeks and the startled desire in her gaze. More than anything he'd ever wanted in his life, Roman wanted to rip the clothes from her body and pleasure her until she came apart in his arms.

And then do it again and again.

As they gazed at each other, the moment seemed suspended in time. Even dressed like a scruffy boy, Antonia was beautiful—a gift from the fairy realm, sweetly magical. Far too good for a cynical, soul-blackened bastard like him.

Roman also knew without a doubt that she would be his.

"All right?" he asked softly.

Her smile trembled like a butterfly's wings. "Better than all right."

"Excellent. Shut your eyes, love."

She obeyed, her eyelids drifting closed as he teased her sex with long, lingering strokes. Antonia shifted restlessly in his lap, soft, excited whimpers falling from her lips. Roman bent and covered her mouth with his, swallowing the delicious sounds.

Just as he parted her, ready to slip a finger inside her sweet body, incoherent yelling from outside the grotto penetrated his sensual haze. Running footsteps pounded by and then receded back into the night.

Hell and damnation.

He'd been so intent on Antonia that any blackguard could have snuck up on them.

Roman tipped her upright in his lap. "It's not safe here anymore. We've got to go."

"Just when things were getting good," she said with a sigh.

He set her on her feet and began restoring order to her appearance. "Sorry about that."

"I'm sure it's not more dangerous than it was a few moments ago," she groused.

He had to bite back a smile. That she'd been clearly enjoying herself spoke well of their future.

"Maybe, but there are lawmen everywhere, and one of them is bound to stumble upon us sooner or later. I won't have you discovered like this."

She let out a derisive snort.

"Besides," he added, "think of poor Richard. He's probably frantic with worry."

"You don't give a hang about Richard, but I'm afraid you're right. If he can't find me, he'll do something drastic."

"Such as?" He took her hand and stepped cautiously out of the grotto.

"He'll probably go to my father. Or to his father, which would be the same thing, because Mr. Keane would fetch Papa. There would be a scene."

There was going to be a scene anyway, but Roman would handle it. It was just a matter of figuring out the proper strategy.

"With luck, we'll get you home before Richard shows up. Just pull your hat down and don't talk."

"Why can't I talk?"

He led her in the direction of the water entrance of the Gardens, where they could hire a boat. "Because, sweetheart, you sound nothing like a man."

He caught the flash of her smile. "Are you sure about that?" she asked in a credibly gruff voice.

"You're incorrigible."

"But you like me anyway, don't you?"

Doubt lurked underneath the cheery tone. Roman pulled her into the shadows of an oak and swept her into his arms, planting a heated and very thorough kiss on her mouth.

"Does that answer your question?" he said as he pulled back.

She had to clear her throat. "Yes, thank you."

"Good. Now let's hurry before we run into any more trouble."

As luck would have it, they made their way to the water entrance with no further alarms. The crisis had obviously passed. The fight had concluded as well, evidenced by the revelers heading to the dock, excitedly parsing Emperor's upset victory over

King. Roman quickly secured a boat to ferry Antonia and him across the river.

"That was easy," she said a few minutes later as he helped her out of the skiff and up the steps leading to the street. "Richard and I usually go round by the road, but I'll be sure to take a boat to Vauxhall from now on."

"You will not," Roman said as he hailed a hackney. "Unless you're coming as a proper young lady with a proper escort."

"Killjoy," she muttered.

He gave the driver the address and climbed in after her. "Do we really need to have a discussion about this?"

She flapped a hand. "You needn't worry. I've already decided I'm getting too old for this sort of escapade."

"You never should have started in the first place."

She twisted on the narrow seat to study him. "Does it bother you that much?"

"Only because you put yourself in harm's way, love. But that's not the real question, is it?"

"I...no, it's not."

"You want to know if I understand *why* you did it."

"You're very quick," she said approvingly. "I quite like that about you."

"Thank you," he said dryly. "Antonia, I do understand. It's not been easy for you, given the rumors you've had to contend with since your real father came back into your life."

"They're not rumors."

"You're expected to behave with a great deal of decorum, and are judged even more severely than most young ladies. That sort of burden can be wearisome, so it's understandable you'd kick over the traces now and again."

She rewarded him with a warm smile. "Exactly. No doubt you've had to deal with your share of rumors and gossip, too."

"It's different for a man."

"Especially the son of a prince."

"A fact which has its disadvantages, believe me."

Her golden gaze twinkled with mischief. "How sad for you, dear sir."

He shook his head. "You can be quite the brat when you put your mind to it."

"It's a talent." She glanced out the window as they pulled into Kensington Square. "Confound it, we're almost to my house. I forgot to tell the driver to stop before we got here."

When she started to pound on the ceiling, he grabbed her arm. "That won't be necessary."

"Are you mad? I've got to sneak through the back garden and up to my room without anyone seeing me."

"Have you forgotten Richard?"

She winced. "Maybe he has yet to arrive. I can keep an eye out from my room and whistle if I see him coming down the street, to warn him off."

When the carriage rolled to a stop, he opened the door and handed her down. "It doesn't matter, because I'm coming in with you."

She dug in her heels in front of the Barnett family's elegant-looking house. "Papa will kill you."

"That is a chance I will have to take." He nudged her up the steps.

"Why are you doing this?" she asked in an almost panicked tone.

"Because I'm going to ask for Captain and Mrs. Barnett's permission to court you. Formally. No more getting abducted or sneaking about in dirty grottos."

When she gaped at him, Roman took the opportunity to give the doorknocker a smart rap.

A black-garbed butler opened the door, his eyes widening as he took in Antonia's outfit. "Oh, miss, thank the good Lord," he said in a relieved voice.

"I'm absolutely fine, Preston," she said.

"Of course. May I take your, er, cap?"

With a commendable degree of insouciance, she removed her disreputable headgear and handed it over. "I take it Richard is here."

"Yes, miss. He arrived—"

"Antonia!"

Captain Barnett charged down the stairs like an enraged bull. Roman was about to yank Antonia to safety when she mounted her own charge, running straight into her father's arms.

"It's all right, Papa." Her voice was muffled against his coat. "I'm fine."

Barnett hugged her back. "Are you sure?" he asked in a choked voice.

"Perfectly sure."

He put her at arm's length. "What the devil were you thinking to place yourself in such danger? And why didn't you stay with Richard when all hell broke loose?"

"We got separated in the crowd. Roman…Captain Cantrell…found me and was kind enough to escort me home."

Barnett finally seemed to register Roman's presence—with a scowl, naturally. He looked at his daughter again, his gaze turning suspicious.

"He simply looked after me, Papa. Truly."

"He didn't take advantage of you in any way?"

She patted her father's chest, as if trying to calm an excitable guard dog. "Indeed not."

Roman had to admire her talent for prevarication. But something *had* happened, and he had every intention of taking advantage of it.

"Is that true?" Barnett asked, glaring at Roman.

"For the most part," he replied. "Of necessity, we were alone for several minutes in a grotto in the woods."

Antonia looked ready to shoot him. "It was nothing," she said through clenched teeth.

Barnett followed her look. "I'm going to kill you, Cantrell. That's a promise."

"I hope not in the entrance hall, my dear," Mrs. Barnett said from where she'd quietly stationed herself at the foot of the stairs. "Good evening, Captain Cantrell."

He bowed. "Ma'am, it's a pleasure to see you."

She gave him a slight smile. "We'll see about that."

"How can you be calm about this, Marissa?" Barnett said. "Antonia could have been killed. Or worse."

"Oh, good Lord," his daughter muttered.

"Not according to Richard," Mrs. Barnett replied. "He told us the captain had secured Antonia, did he not?"

Roman glanced up to see Richard sidling down the stairs. He edged his way around the group and made his way to the door.

"Well, I'll just toddle off," the young man said in a dementedly cheerful tone. "Now that Tony's safely home, all's well that ends well."

"No thanks to you," Barnett said. "Our discussion is not finished, Richard. And I *will* be talking to your father."

Richard deflated like a punctured soufflé. "Yes, sir."

Antonia scowled at her friend as he hotfooted his way out the door.

"As for you, miss," her father started.

"Not in the hall, Anthony," his wife said firmly. She herded Antonia up the staircase like an errant lamb, clearly expecting the men to follow.

"After you, Captain Cantrell," Barnett said in a soft but lethal tone.

Roman followed the ladies, half-expecting Antonia's father to plunge a knife between his shoulder blades.

Mrs. Barnett led them along a thickly carpeted hall to an elegant but comfortably furnished drawing room at the back of the house. There were flowers in pretty vases, several embroidery frames, and books piled on tables. It was a room that felt lived in by people who enjoyed each other's company.

It was an unfamiliar concept to him. His mother had never truly recovered from the scandal of his birth, and for much of his youth, he'd been more of an embarrassment to his family than a blessing.

When they were seated, Barnett leveled a severe look at his daughter. "Start at the beginning, and tell us everything that happened tonight."

Antonia proceeded to give a barebones and laughably mild version, making it sound as harmless as a stroll in Hyde Park. Mention of the grotto was noticeably absent.

"It was really just a lark with Richard," she said, finishing up. "I'm sorry I made such a mess of things."

"Naturally, we're displeased, Antonia," her mother said, "but it could have been much worse. We must be thankful that Captain Cantrell was at hand."

"I suppose we must," said Barnett. "But what about that blasted grotto? Something obviously went on there."

"It was nothing, Papa," Antonia said with a vague wave.

Roman was beginning to find that particular answer annoying. "I'm afraid I can't agree. We were alone in there for at least fifteen minutes."

Her wince was slight but noticeable. "Yes, but no one saw us."

"Someone is not telling the truth here," Barnett said sternly.

Might as well let it rip, old son. "Sir, although my primary goal was getting your daughter safely home," Roman said, "I had another reason for wishing to speak with you and Mrs. Barnett."

"And that is?"

"To ask for your permission to court your daughter."

"That tears it," Antonia muttered.

Her mother tried to cover a sudden smile, but Barnett's jaw sagged open.

"What?" he finally managed.

"I'd like to court Miss Barnett, with the intention of marrying her," Roman carefully enunciated.

Barnett leapt to his feet. "You must be joking! I'll keelhaul you before I allow you to touch my daughter."

"Papa!" Antonia exclaimed, also jumping up.

"Did you agree to this demented scheme?" her father demanded. "Have you said yes to this bounder?"

"Of course not."

When Roman started to protest, she held up a restraining hand. "But I like Captain Cantrell very much, and I can't think of any sensible reason why he should not court me. It's not as if he has a lot of competition, you know."

"Only because men are generally idiots," Roman said. "I, however, am not."

Mrs. Barnett applauded. "Good for you, Captain."

Her husband groaned. "Please don't tell me you agree with them, Marissa. You have no idea how bad this is."

"Then why don't you sit down and tell us, because the captain seems like a perfectly decent man to me." She hesitated. "Although I cannot approve of that earring, I must say."

"I can get rid of it." Roman mostly wore it to annoy his disapproving family.

"But I like it," Antonia protested.

"You're missing the point," Barnett growled. "The man's simply not fit for you."

"Papa, I'm quite tired of such vague assertions," she said impatiently. "You need to be clear if you want me to understand."

"Very well, then. I wanted to spare you, but that's clearly no longer possible."

Roman braced himself for what was coming next.

"Cantrell is a ruthless killer," Barnett said, "and I won't allow you to marry a man who is all but a criminal. Also, I have little doubt he only wishes to marry you to get his hands on Nightingale Trading."

Antonia, obviously stunned by the accusations, grimaced with pain at her father's last comment.

"Anthony, stop," warned his wife.

"I suppose it would never occur to you that a man should wish to marry me for my own sake," Antonia said in a flat tone.

Now her father winced and shook his head. "That's not what I meant, my dearest girl. Any decent, worthy fellow would be happy to marry you."

"Apparently most fellows do not share your opinion." She scrunched her nose, as if trying to hold back tears.

"Antonia, I'd want you even if your father disowned you," Roman said. "You're beautiful, both inside and out."

"You have no idea what she needs, Cantrell," Barnett snapped.

"No, but she does. She's smart enough and sensible enough to think for herself."

"Thank you, Captain," she said with a glimmer of a smile. "And since I can indeed make up my own mind, I would be grateful if you could respond to Papa's accusations."

Well, he'd walked right into that one. "The one where he all but called me a murderer?"

"Yes, let's hear about that," Barnett said sarcastically.

"Papa, please be quiet. And do sit down."

When her father subsided with a mutter, Antonia nodded at Roman.

"I already told you that I captained a privateering vessel during the war," he said.

Barnett scowled. "A pirate vessel."

His wife whacked his shoulder. "Be quiet, Anthony. Please continue, Captain."

"Thank you, ma'am. You also know that privateers and manned merchantmen are bound by the same rules of war as British naval ships."

"Yes, if you capture an enemy vessel, its crew is entitled to decent treatment as prisoners of war," Antonia said.

"If the captives are not treated humanely, then the Admiralty Courts can revoke a ship's letter of marque and refuse to award any prize money. In the most egregious cases, monetary damages can be leveled against the ship's officers and crew."

"Or they can be hanged if found guilty of murder," Barnett said in a hard voice.

"Yes," Roman said. "But I was cleared of such charges."

"Only because your father is a bloody royal duke and an admiral," Barnett said.

"No, because the charges weren't true."

"Details, please," Antonia said impatiently.

Roman kept his voice level, even though he loathed what he had to say. "Two years ago, we captured an enemy ship off the coast of Africa. It was a French merchantman, well armed. The crew was no match for us, but in the fighting several of my men died, including my first mate and my surgeon."

"That's awful," she said softly.

"It was. Afterward, my crew was stretched thin, and that led to an incident on board the merchantman after it had been secured." He pressed his lips together for a moment, but there was no sugarcoating it. "A few of my men killed several of the French officers."

"Slaughtered them, you mean," Barnett said.

Antonia and her mother exchanged distressed glances.

"It happened during an escape attempt, although that hardly excuses their actions," Roman said.

"Where were you when all this occurred?" Antonia asked.

"Sick as a dog in my cabin. I'd been felled by an infection a few days earlier. My second mate was in command during the incident on the French ship." Sam Wilson, an intelligent but hot-tempered man, had led the killing himself.

She sagged in her chair with relief. "So, it wasn't really your fault."

"*Everything* that takes place on a ship is the responsibility of the captain," said Barnett. "You know that."

"But—"

"Your father is correct," Roman said. "I gave my crew the order to attack the enemy ship, even though I couldn't supervise the battle or the aftermath."

He'd done it because the prize was too rich to pass up. And he'd been sure his crew was up to the task.

He'd been wrong about them, especially Wilson.

Antonia's grimace was sympathetic. "It sounds terrible, but I still don't understand why anyone would think you personally guilty of murder."

"Partly because of what came later," Barnett said grimly. "Shall I tell them?"

Roman ignored him to focus on Antonia. "I became aware of the magnitude of the incident when I came out of a bout of fever. When I relieved my second officer and ordered him confined to quarters, he challenged my order."

"What did you do?" she whispered.

"We fought and I killed him." With a desperate knife to the throat, something he'd never forget. He'd been so weakened by illness that he still wondered how he'd managed to save himself.

When Antonia went deathly still and pale, Roman had to resist the impulse to snatch her into his arms to comfort her. She'd probably push him away if he did—or Barnett would toss him through the window.

"I had no choice," he went on. "It was either that or lose control of my ship."

And lose his life. Almost half of his crew had sided with the mutinous second mate.

"A good captain never loses control of his vessel," said Barnett. "That the situation developed in the first place was your fault."

"I do not disagree with that assessment." Roman had failed to see how ragged his crew was, and how close they were to the edge after months at sea. At war.

"Then you agree that you are neither a fit captain nor a fit husband for my daughter."

Antonia came back to life. "Papa, that's for me to decide, at least when it comes to the latter."

Her father rose, his expression hardening into relentless determination.

Oh, hell.

"No, it is not," said Barnett. "You have only one choice, Antonia. It's him or us."

"What?" Antonia and Mrs. Barnett echoed, their tones equally aghast.

"You heard me. It's Cantrell, or your family. You cannot have both."

"Anthony, have you gone mad?" exclaimed his wife.

He flashed her an impatient look. "Marissa, I'm trying to save our daughter."

Antonia jumped to her feet and grabbed her father's arm. "I cannot believe you would force such a dreadful choice on me. Think of the way you and Mamma were so cruelly separated by my grandfather all those years ago. How can you even think to do the same thing to me?"

Barnett flinched, but quickly recovered. "The situations are entirely different, Antonia. Your mother and I had loved each other for years before we were forced apart. You barely know Cantrell, so it shouldn't be a difficult choice to make."

She stared up at her father, looking so wounded and lost that Roman swore someone had just slammed a fist into his heart.

With a weary sigh, he stood. "It's not a choice I would force you to make, either, Antonia."

He took her small, cold hand. She clutched at him. "I'm sorry, sweetheart. I never wished to cause you such distress. I hope you can forgive me."

"Roman," she whispered.

He let go her hand and quickly left the room.

CHAPTER SIX

Antonia's father and the Duke of Clarence sat side by side in the spacious Vauxhall supper box that overlooked the extravagant grand ball closing out the Regent's birthday festivities.

"They don't look happy," Antonia said to Justine Steele, who sat with her on the opposite side of the box.

"Stupendously disgruntled I'd say, but that is often the case when receiving a lecture from Sir Dominic Hunter," replied Justine. "Although beneficial, it is rarely enjoyable."

Antonia had never been formally introduced to the powerful magistrate before tonight. But thanks to his wife's urgings, Sir Dominic had agreed to intervene on Roman's behalf. Unfortunately, Papa had dug in his heels, and she doubted anything short of an Act of Parliament would budge him. Since it seemed the duke was equally opposed to any talk of marriage, the situation seemed hopeless.

"It's awkward, isn't it? Of course, it's an honor to spend an evening in one of the royal boxes, but..."

"Awkward describes it perfectly," Justine said dryly.

The duke had given Antonia a stern inspection before responding brusquely to her curtsy. Papa had bristled in response. He might not want her marrying Clarence's son, but no one snubbed his daughter, not even a prince. The duke obviously struggled with a similar dilemma. He was opposed to the marriage but annoyed that anyone, especially a commoner, should find Roman lacking.

If Antonia wasn't so dreadfully upset by the events of the last few days, she might even find amusement in the ridiculous situation.

"I'm sorry His Grace was so short-tempered with you," Justine said. "He's normally quite the friendliest of all the King's sons."

Antonia tried to pretend it didn't matter. "He was very nice to Mamma, though, and I know he's always gotten along well with Papa, since they're both sailors. But I honestly don't know why he invited us tonight, since he clearly disapproves of me as a potential wife for Roman."

"You can thank Sir Dominic. It was his suggestion."

"It was kind of him, but I'm not sure why he would go through all the trouble."

"Because Chloe approves of you." Justine smiled. "As do the rest of us, I might add."

"Except for the fathers," Antonia said.

"Sir Dominic hopes to effect a positive change."

"Good luck with that. Even Mamma can't get through to my father." She heaved a sigh. "Not that it matters, since Roman has no intention of courting me after all."

Antonia still couldn't believe he'd given up so easily. But perhaps he'd seen it as an opportunity. After their unexpected and torrid encounter in the grotto, he'd probably felt duty-bound to make an offer for her. Papa's grandiose threat had then opened the door for him to walk away.

Unfortunately, she had no doubts regarding her feelings for Roman. She was in love with the blasted man, for all the good it would do her.

"Not true," Justine said. "Roman is head over heels for you. Chloe thinks so, too."

Antonia had to swallow twice before she could answer. "While I'd like to believe that's true, I can't seem to shake the awful sensation that Roman only offered for me because his honor demanded it."

"My husband found himself in a similar position when he offered for me."

That seemed hard to believe. "Really?"

"Yes. But understand that no one forces men like Roman or my husband to do anything against their wishes. If Roman proposed, it's because he truly wants to marry you."

Antonia splayed her hands wide. "Then why did he just storm out the other night?"

Justine glanced to the front of the box, where Papa and the duke were now engaged in a tense but fairly civil discussion. Sir Dominic loomed over them, regarding the fathers as a schoolmaster would watch over disobedient schoolboys—in other words, ready to box their ears if they stepped out of line.

She returned her attention to Antonia. "Roman suggested to us that your father delivered an ultimatum."

"Yes, it was a hideous moment. Papa said I had to choose between Roman, or him and Mamma."

"That's the explanation, I think. Roman would never wish to put you in such a terrible position. He knows how much you love your parents."

"It was an empty threat. Papa would never throw me off, no matter how angry he got. Even so, Roman should have trusted me to make my own decision."

Justine wrinkled her nose. "I agree. But men like Roman and my husband find it difficult to trust. They suffered a great deal of rejection and heartache when they were young, and that sort of experience is hard to overcome. I think you understand, don't you?"

"Yes, I certainly do," Antonia said wryly. She'd also been subject to rejection and disapproval by the man she'd thought her real father, and then by the *beau monde*, who deemed her a walking scandal by virtue of her parentage.

"Roman's pride would never allow him to show his pain to the world, so he built up a hard shell in order to defend himself."

"I did the same," Antonia confessed. "I either pretended all the insults didn't hurt, or I made a joke out of them. But it's not easy living like that."

"And men are so very bad at admitting that they might not be right about everything, especially when it comes to their own emotions."

"But how do you get someone like that to change?"

"Well, I find that men are rather like nuts. You must splinter that hard shell of theirs to get to the good bits."

"That sounds vaguely improper."

"I find that nothing gets through to a man better than a bit of improper behavior. Judiciously and discretely applied, it can work wonders."

Antonia had to laugh. "That's all well and good, but I can hardly engage in naughty behavior with my parents and the Duke of Clarence hanging about. Besides, Roman is noticeably absent. I can't even talk to him, much less drag him off into the woods for a spot of illicit activity."

"Actually, he's right over there, to the side of the orchestra pavilion."

When she spotted the tall, broad-shouldered figure dressed in black, Antonia's thoughts scattered like puffballs in the wind. It took her a moment to gather her wits.

"What's he doing over there?" Then she sighed. "I hope he's not avoiding me."

"He and Griffin are up to something, as far as I can tell. They disappeared before you and your parents arrived, much to the irritation of the duke."

"He does seem to be lurking about in a suspicious fashion, doesn't he?"

"Yes, which is why I think you should go over there and get to the bottom of things. And if you stumble across my husband, please tell him I'd like a word with him."

Antonia wavered. "I…I don't know if I should. My parents won't like it."

Justine's eyebrows lifted with polite incredulity. "I don't believe you ever let that stop you before, did you?"

"Well, no."

"Your mother and Chloe are still strolling around the Grove, and Dominic has gone back to lecturing the fathers. So, it's the perfect time to speak to Roman. If, that is, you can find the courage."

"That sounds like a dare to me," Antonia said.

Justine simply smiled.

Antonia had never thought of herself as a coward, and she wasn't about to start now. "I'll be right back."

***

Roman glanced over his shoulder into the wooded thicket. Griffin was back there somewhere with a few of his men, keeping watch over the jostling crowd. It was a mad crush, with half the idiots in London determined to wring every ounce of enjoyment out of the lavish ending to the Regent's celebrations.

Tonight would be worth the trouble if his target revealed himself. Roman could then get back to convincing Antonia to marry him. That's what this gambit was all about—a chance to correct his blunders. With luck and a little help from Dominic and Griffin, he intended to do just that.

If Antonia still wanted him. After the sordid tale she heard the other night, she might well decide that a blackguard like him wasn't worth the trouble, especially if marriage could destroy the relationship with her parents. Still, he just couldn't give up on her. Give up on *them*. If there was to be any hope for a successful outcome, he had to prove to Barnett that he could protect and cherish her.

And then he had to prove to Antonia that he was worthy of her—or at least that he would spend the rest of his life *trying* to be worthy of her. If only the blasted—

A jab to the shoulder interrupted his thoughts. He didn't know whether to laugh or curse, knowing exactly who he would see when he turned around.

Antonia stood calmly before him. She was dressed in a silvery-blue gown that emphasized her dainty figure, and so pretty that it made his chest ache. It took considerable willpower to refrain from pulling her into his arms and kissing her until she agreed to marry him. The wary expression in her eyes, however, suggested an attempt at a torrid embrace would not be the best of strategies.

"You might try saying hello, for once," he said. "It's a surprisingly effective way to get a man's attention."

"Perhaps I'll try that when I'm not annoyed with you."

Out of the corner of his eye, Roman caught a glimpse of Griffin, shaking his head in warning before fading back into the deep shadows of the trees. "You can be as annoyed with me as you want when we're back in my father's supper box. I'll join you there shortly."

She frowned. "Are you trying to get rid of me?"

"Of course not. This is simply not a convenient place to talk."

"And trying to have an intimate discussion in front of our fathers is?"

"Antonia—"

"Why are you lurking about under the trees? You look suspicious."

"I'm meeting someone."

"Who?"

"You don't need to know."

The light in her golden gaze snuffed out. "Then I'll leave you alone, sir."

He grabbed her arm. "Come back here, you daft girl. It's nothing like that."

Her shaky sigh confirmed his suspicions.

"Antonia, do you really think I would sneak off to an assignation with another woman? After what's happened between us?"

Her shoulders lifted in an awkward shrug. "I don't know what to think. You were rather quick to bolt the other night."

"I know, sweetheart, and that was badly done of me. But I was taken aback by your father's ultimatum."

"It was quite hideous but mostly bluster. Papa would never be so cruel."

"Are you so sure? Your father thinks I'm a menace."

"He doesn't know you like I do."

Her quiet expression of confidence affected him oddly, as if some part of his internal anatomy was shifting. While he struggled with the unfamiliar feeling, she rested a slim hand on his arm. "Roman, do you trust me?"

"Of course. You're the most trustworthy person I've ever met."

"Even though I sneak about dressed as a boy and attend prizefights?"

"You do have a talent for prevarication, love, but you only shade the truth to protect the people you care about. And you never let anyone force you to be something you're not, even if it would make life easier. I admire you for that more than I can say."

She pressed a hand to her chest and flashed him a misty smile. "Oh, Roman. That's…amazing. You're amazing."

Instead of basking in the glow of her approval, he adopted a stern expression. "Which doesn't mean I want you fibbing to me, Antonia. I know who you are and what you need, and I'm fine with it."

"And I would say the same. You don't have to insulate me from what happened to you during the war. I'm strong enough to take it."

"Take the fact that I'm a killer?"

Her mouth scrunched sideways. "What would have happened if you hadn't defended yourself?"

"I would have ended up with a knife in my gut and tossed into the sea."

"I think we can agree that would have been a remarkably bad outcome."

"Indeed," he said dryly.

"As for your crew, what would have happened to them?"

"They'd have been charged with mutiny."

"Yes, which would have led to even more deaths." She studied him for a few moments. "I know you hate talking about this, but you need to see that incident for what it truly was."

"An epic disaster?" he said, taking refuge in sarcasm.

"An impossible situation," she quietly replied.

He sighed. "You're right, of course, but your father was also right when he said that I made the decisions that led to the final outcome. It was my ship and my command, ergo my fault."

"And like a good ship's captain, did you not accept responsibility for those events?"

He tried to be fair to himself. "I hope I did."

"Of course you did. You were vindicated by the Admiralty Court."

"That line of argumentation didn't convince your father, though."

"Papa was wrong. We both know that."

He wanted to believe her. "Do we?"

Antonia rolled her eyes. "Roman, do you truly think of yourself as a murderer?"

"No."

"Then for heaven's sake, learn to forgive yourself, even if others cannot."

"Easier said than done," he said gruffly. "Especially with your father acting like I'm some sort of monster out to ravish his darling daughter."

"That sounds rather fun," she said with a grin.

"Antonia—"

"Roman, hang what anybody else thinks, including my father. All you need to worry about is how you and I feel about it."

He finally gave in to impulse and took her hand. For such a little thing, she had a surprisingly sturdy grip. "And have you forgiven me?"

"There's nothing to forgive—except for the way you flounced out of our drawing room in that excessively dramatic fashion. I hardly knew where to look."

He wanted to laugh and take her into his arms, spinning her around until they were both dizzy. It was a silly, boyish impulse, and it felt wonderful. "Pirates are supposed to flounce around like idiots. But are you sure, Antonia? There will be talk, possibly even a scandal, if we marry."

"We're both used to that, which probably makes us perfect for each other."

She was perfect for him, but he wasn't sure she fully realized the challenges they were likely to face.

When he didn't answer right away, she let out an exasperated sigh. "Roman, do you love me?"

Ah, that was an easy one. "I started falling in love with you that first moment when you marched across the Grove to put your father and me in our places."

"Then everything will be all right, because I love you, too. I won't allow anyone to separate us. I'll run them through with a rusty blade if they try."

Her comically fierce and wonderfully stubborn love swept away his last shred of resistance. All that was left now was the feeling that everything he'd ever wanted was finally close at hand.

"Not our fathers, though," he said with a grin. "That would put a ghastly crimp in the wedding plans."

"I'll make an exception for those two—if they don't annoy me too much."

"Splendid." He resisted the impulse to kiss her with a full measure of passion, instead dropping a quick kiss on her adorable nose.

She smiled up at him. "Now are you ready to break the news to our parents?"

Good God.

He'd completely lost track of time—and why he was lurking under this tree in the first place. "Antonia, you need to return to the box right now. I'll join you soon, I promise."

"Why can't you come with me now?"

"I'll explain later. Please go."

Her gaze narrowed. "Roman, what's going on?"

"Nothing. It's—" A pistol jabbed him between the shoulder blades. "Oh, hell."

Antonia's eyes popped wide with understanding and consternation.

"Back up now," growled a voice in his ear. "You and the girl both."

Roman backed them deep into the copse before turning around. He got a jolt when he saw an elderly man who should be snoozing in front of the hearth, not holding people up. But although the fellow was stoop-shouldered and wizened, his hand was steady and his gaze glittered with cold, calculating intent.

"Who the hell are you?" Roman asked.

"You killed my grandson, Sam, and I'll have what you owe me for that."

"Sam Wilson," Roman growled. His second mate on the *Mary Lynn*.

Antonia let out a small gasp. "You mean..."

"Aye, that's the one," the old man snarled. "The one he murdered."

"Sir, I am so sorry for your loss, but the captain didn't murder your grandson or anyone else," Antonia said.

"Please let me handle this," Roman said.

"There ain't nothing to handle, Cantrell," the man said. "You need to pay up for what you did to me and mine."

Roman frowned at the odd phrasing. "Pay up? You want money?"

The old man's craggy features suddenly froze. Griffin had just materialized from behind a tree and was no doubt pressing the barrel of *his* pistol against the fellow's back.

"I suspect this gentleman is, in fact, willing to take financial compensation for the loss of his grandson," Griffin said in a dry tone.

Antonia rounded on Roman. "You set this up, didn't you? You used yourself as bait."

Roman shrugged. "I needed to know who was threatening me."

"That was incredibly foolhardy, not to mention dangerous. I cannot believe you took such a risk."

"There was no risk," Griffin said. "My plans are always foolproof."

"He could have shot Roman without saying a word. You're both idiots," she snapped.

"Love, you can berate us all you want later, but we do have to deal with this situation," Roman said.

"Just kill me and get it over with," the old man said bitterly. "That's what you do, ain't it?"

"No, it's not what I do," said Roman. "If I could have found another way to manage the situation on my ship, I would have done so. Sam took the choice out of my hands by promoting mutiny."

The grandfather's wrinkled features sagged with genuine grief. "Aye, he could be rash. Took after me, the foolish lad. But he supported us, me and his aunts. And now we have nothin', not even his pension to go on."

Roman's second mate had never breathed a word about his family. "Sir, I am truly sorry you've been forced to bear such hardship. I will arrange compensation to replace your grandson's income." And then some.

The old man looked flummoxed. "Why?"

"Because your grandson's death was a tragedy for all involved." Roman glanced at Griffin. "You'll take care of the details?"

"I'll work it out and talk to you later," his cousin said.

Roman directed a stern look at the old man. "Do I have your word that this will be the end of it? Your family will not threaten me or mine again?"

"Oh, I'll be talking to Mr. Wilson's family," Griffin said, clamping a hand on the fellow's shoulder. "My men already have your inept co-conspirators under guard not far from here."

"They just be my wife's cousins," the grandfather said in a surly tone. "They was helpin' me get my due, that's all."

"Their help will no longer be required," Griffin said, marching him away into the night.

"Griffin won't hurt him, will he?" Antonia asked rather anxiously.

Roman guided her toward the Grove. "No, but he'll put the fear of God into him. He and his family won't trouble us again."

She sighed. "Not that I approve of his actions, but I couldn't help feeling sorry for the old fellow."

"I'll make sure the Wilsons are taken care of."

She hugged his arm. "You're a good man, Captain Cantrell. I'm so glad you *finally* agreed to marry me."

He laughed. "Sweetheart, it's only been a few weeks since we met. This has hardly been a lengthy courtship."

"I feel like I've been waiting for you for such a long time."

"It's the same for me." It was rather a miracle.

"Then the sooner we get married, the better, don't you think?" she asked.

"I do."

She gave an endearing little skip of joy. "Oh, good."

As he escorted her through the festive throng, Roman pondered the unfamiliar feeling settling deep in his core. It took a few minutes before he realized what it was—unadulterated happiness.

The splendid sensation abated just a jot as they approached the supper box. His father and Barnett sat side by side, a study in parental disgruntlement. Dominic and the ladies were gathered on the opposite side of the box, as if putting as much distance from them as possible.

"Oh, dear," said Antonia. "They don't look any happier than when I left."

"I don't suppose you would consider eloping, would you?" Roman asked. "Immediately."

"At least they're not yelling at each other."

"And the women seem calm, so it would appear Dominic's machinations had a positive effect on at least some of our relatives."

"Mamma will be quite happy to welcome you as a son-in-law."

Roman threw her a skeptical glance as he led her up to the box. "Really?"

"Yes. Then I become your problem, not hers," she said with a twinkle.

He swallowed a laugh when both Clarence and Barnett turned to them with almost identical scowls.

"Antonia, what did I tell you about sneaking off?" her father said. "You're supposed to be staying out of trouble, not actively seeking it."

"She was with my son," said Clarence. "Miss Barnett was perfectly safe with him."

Let the prevaricating begin.

"That's absolutely correct," Antonia said. "*Perfectly* safe. Roman and I were just having a little chat."

"You didn't happen to stumble across my husband, did you?" Justine asked.

Antonia winced. "Oh, I forgot to mention that you wanted to speak with him."

"He'll be along at some point, I imagine," Roman said.

Justine simply rolled her eyes.

"So that's it, I suppose," Clarence said with a dramatic sigh. "You're going to marry the girl."

"I rather thought I would, sir," said Roman.

"If it means Dominic will cease badgering me, it's worth it," his father replied.

"I never badger, Your Grace. I simply suggest," Dominic said.

Barnett let out a sardonic snort but refrained from comment.

"Oh, well, at least you're a seaman's daughter," Clarence said to Antonia. Then he seemed to brighten. "And your father *is* very rich, so I'm sure he'll give you a splendid dowry." He elbowed the long-suffering Barnett in the ribs. "Won't you, old man?"

"If you think—"

"Antonia will indeed receive a splendid dowry, Your Grace," Mrs. Barnett cut in. "And we'll be honored to welcome Captain Cantrell into our family." She gave Roman a warm, welcoming smile. "I've always wanted a son."

Roman's throat went a bit tight. "Thank you, ma'am, but the honor is truly all mine."

"Neatly done, my boy," said Clarence. He eyed Antonia again and then shrugged. "Well, come give your future papa-in-law a hug, young lady."

Though her eyes went wide, she recovered quickly and did as Clarence requested. She emerged from his embrace looking flustered but happy.

Her happiness dimmed when she took in her father's morose expression.

"I don't like it," Barnett said, casting a sharp glance around. "There's bound to be a great deal of unpleasant talk, given Cantrell's reputation. The London gossips will have a field day with this. It won't be easy."

Since people nearby were practically falling out of their boxes to eavesdrop, no one tried to refute the assertion.

Antonia took her father's hand. "My reputation isn't exactly the best, either, Papa. And I don't need easy. I need happy, like you and Mamma are."

"You can do better," Barnett said stubbornly.

Clarence starched up. "See here, I'll not have you insulting my son."

Mrs. Barnett sighed. "Really, Anthony."

"I'm simply trying to do what's best for Antonia," Barnett protested. "You know she'll run rings around him, and I just want her to be safe."

"Papa, I *will* be safe." Antonia flashed Roman a look full of mischief. "Who better to watch out for me than a ruthless buccaneer?"

"Very true," her mother said. "I'm sure the captain can handle any number of fearsome villains, not to mention the society gossips who snub you."

"Good God," Barnett said in a disgusted tone. "I don't stand a chance, do I?"

"No, and neither did I," Roman said. Not once Antonia had made up her mind, and he thanked God for that. "Might as well give it up."

Barnett eyed him with disfavor but finally muttered a sailor's curse. "Just promise me that you'll be happy with the blackguard," he said to Antonia.

She gave her father a fierce hug. "That's the easiest promise I'll ever make. Thank you, Papa, for trusting me."

"I still say he's not good enough for you," Barnett grumbled.

Roman gave his old rival and future father-in-law a wry look. "I agree. Then again, no one is, so she might as well marry someone who appreciates her for what she is."

Antonia took his hand. "You mean skinny, short, and more than slightly odd?" she asked in a teasing voice.

Roman looked into her enchanting face, her joy lighting up his heart. Finally and at long last, he'd arrived in safe harbor.

"No," he said. "I mean perfect. Absolutely perfect."

**KEEP READING FOR AN EXCERPT
FROM VANESSA'S NEXT RELEASE,
*THE HIGHLANDER WHO PROTECTED ME
CLAN KENDRICK 1***

CHAPTER ONE OF
THE HIGHLANDER WHO PROTECTED
ME
CLAN KENDRICK BOOK ONE

Bestselling author Vanessa Kelly returns with an enthralling new series about the men of the Kendrick clan—and the women who claim their hearts . . .

Lady Ainsley Matthews, heiress and darling of the *ton*, was expected to make a magnificent match. Instead she's hiding on a remote Scottish estate, terrified that her vicious former fiancé will use her pregnancy to force her into marriage. One man can help her—Royal Kendrick, son of a distinguished Highland clan. Though a mistake drove them apart long ago, Royal is the only person Ainsley trusts to protect her baby—even if that means agreeing to never see either of them again . . .

Scarred in body and soul by war, Royal suddenly has a purpose—caring for an innocent babe and thereby helping the woman he can't stop loving. But when Ainsley ultimately returns to Scotland, determined to be a real mother to her child in spite of the risk, there's only one solution: marriage. And only one likely outcome: surrendering to the desire that's simmered between them for so long, no matter how dangerous it may be . . .

Clan Kendrick, a new series spinning off from The Highlander's Princess Bride (Improper Princesses 3)

***

Chapter 1

Castle Kinglas, Scotland
April, 1817

Clearly, not even his brother's library could provide safe haven.

With a sigh, Royal glanced up from his book when his sister-in-law marched into the room. Though the former Victoria Knight was now Countess of Arnprior, and wife to the chief of Clan Kendrick, she was still very much a governess in spirit and looked ready to box his ears.

He raised a polite eyebrow. "Is there something I can do for you, my lady?"

She ached an eloquent brow in return. Perhaps they could conduct this sure-to-be-unpleasant discussion entirely through facial expressions.

No such luck, he thought, when Victoria raised an imperious finger.

"Indeed there is. I want you to stop moping about the castle. You've been doing it all winter, and it's become ridiculous."

She was never one to mince words or shy away from an unpleasant task. And now that she'd sorted out his brothers, she'd clearly made Royal her special project.

"I'm not moping. I'm reading a very good book."

Victoria glanced down at the leather-bound volume, then plucked it from his hand and turned it right side up.

Royal winced. "I was just giving my eyes a rest."

"Of course you were," she said dryly.

He'd barely glanced at the blasted thing, a history of the Punic Wars he'd ordered last month. After starting it with a fair degree of enthusiasm, he'd quickly lost interest. Today, he'd read only a few pages before his attention had wandered to the windswept vista of craggy peaks hulking over the loch behind Kinglas. Not even the dramatic beauty of the Highlands had the power to soothe him—not like it once had.

He supposed he could go fishing, which he normally enjoyed, but that hardly seemed worth the effort.

"At least join us for a cup of tea," Victoria said in a coaxing voice, switching tactics. "Taffy made her special seed cakes for you. She said you barely touched your breakfast. Or your lunch, for that matter."

He glanced over to see a generous tea service set up on the low table in front of the library's fireplace. He hadn't even noticed the footman lug the damn thing in.

His sister-in-law's understanding gaze—along with the fact that Taffy, the castle's housekeeper, thought he needed coddling—triggered an irrational spurt of irritation.

"I'm not one of your pupils, Victoria. Don't try to manage me with promises of treats."

"True. My students invariably displayed better manners."

"She's got you there, old fellow," said Nick from behind the ledgers stacked on his desk. "You *have* been moping about. More than usual, that is. It's time you do something about it."

When Nick and Victoria exchanged furtive glances, Royal had to repress a groan. Clearly, they'd planned this little ambush.

He put his book aside and glared at his older brother with predictably no effect. The Earl of Arnprior was well used to his obstreperous siblings, since he'd all but raised them after the death of their parents. Although the most generous of men, Nick was the proverbial unmovable object when it came to deciding his family's best interests. And once he made a decision, it all but required an Act of Parliament to change it.

"I repeat, I am *not* moping," Royal said. "And don't you have enough to worry about without fretting over me like a granny with gout?"

As usual, Nick was buried under the mountain of work that came with managing the estate, not to mention a large and sometimes fractious Highland clan. Any normal man would founder under the load, but he never failed to rise to the challenge. And now that he'd married Victoria, Nick had finally found the richly deserved happiness so long denied him.

Royal couldn't help feeling envious of having a loving wife *and* a sense of purpose—the feeling that one's life mattered. A compelling reason to wake up in the morning had been lacking in his life for a long time.

Nick had once relied quite heavily on Royal's support for everything from running the estate to managing the younger lads. But Victoria now appropriately filled that role, as well as still tutoring Kade, the youngest Kendrick. The boy had struggled for years with ill health, but under Victoria's loving care, he grew stronger by the day.

Aye, she was a blessing, was the new Countess of Arnprior, though not entirely for Royal. His sister-in-law was as bad as her lord when it came to wanting to repair the broken things around Castle Kinglas, including him.

"And you needn't regard me as if I'm falling into a decline," Royal said to her. "I'm perfectly fine. Better than ever, in fact."

Instead of contradicting that obvious load of bollocks, Victoria smiled. "Of course you are, dear. But I would feel better if you had something to eat."

She held out a hand.

Sighing, he took it, because today he did need help getting to his feet. The pain was always worse in blustery, damp weather. Some days Royal feared he was losing ground with his recovery. Though he faithfully followed the regime of rest and exercise prescribed by the London sawbones, his pain somehow seemed linked to the heaviness in his heart.

"Need help?" Nick asked.

"I'm not a cripple," Royal gritted out, even as he struggled to stand.

"And you know I'm stronger than I look," Victoria said to her husband.

"Aye. Skinny but strong as an ox," Nick said with a grin.

"If that's the sort of compliment you employed to woo the poor girl, it's a wonder Victoria ever married you," Royal said as he found his footing.

Victoria laughed. "That's what my grandfather used to say when I was a young girl hanging about the stables of his coaching inn. I loved helping with the horses."

"He was right," said Royal. "For such a wee *Sassenach*, you're quite hardy."

"I have to be to survive a houseful of wild Highlanders," she cheerfully replied, watching Royal carefully to make sure he wouldn't topple over. "I know. I'm an old mother hen."

When his gaze strayed to the decanters of whisky behind his brother's desk, she waggled a finger. "Tea and something to eat first, Royal."

"Old mother hen is an understatement." He patted her on the shoulder. "You do realize you cannot fix everything, no matter how hard you try."

"I know, and it's just about *killing* me." When he started to laugh, she jabbed him in the arm. "But don't think I'm giving up, either."

"Thank you for the warning."

Nick joined them at the tea table, dropping a quick kiss on his wife's head after she took her seat. "I think we're being a bit hard on you," he said. "You've done a splendid job organizing the family and estate papers, and we all know they were in...quite the state."

"Catastrophic disarray is the phrase you were searching for," Royal said.

"Don't let Angus hear you. He all but flayed me alive when I took the job from him and gave it to you."

"So I heard. My ears are still ringing."

Nick laughed. "Aside from the fact that Angus is a disaster when it comes to paperwork, the old fellow's getting on in years. He's earned his rest."

"I hope to God you didn't tell him so," Royal said. Their grandfather would be devastated if he thought they were putting him out to pasture.

"Since my instincts for self-preservation are quite good, I did not," Nick replied.

When Nick and Royal were away during the war, Angus had managed affairs at Kinglas, watching over the younger Kendricks and serving as estate steward. He'd done his best, but with mixed results. The old fellow had an abiding mistrust of modernity—which to him meant anything after the last Stuart monarch.

"Angus did mention that you did a passable job organizing the papers," Victoria said as she poured them each a cup. "Which from him is high praise, indeed."

"Seriously," Nick said, "I can't thank you enough for taking that on. I know it was gruesome."

Royal shrugged and reached for a seedcake. "I was happy to do so."

Oddly enough, that had turned out to be true. His big brother had dragooned him into taking on the job, determined to get Royal "off his arse."

"You need to accept that your military days are over," Nick had said, adopting his most lordly manner. "It's time to figure out what you wish to do with your life and then simply get on with it."

The problem was, Royal *still* didn't have a clue what he wanted to do.

All he seemed to be good for was mooning over Ainsley Matthews and wondering what might have happened between them if he hadn't been stupid enough to abduct her back in January. He'd kidnapped her with the best of intentions, determined to save her from an arranged marriage she was trying to avoid. Of course, he would have gained the only woman who'd ever made him feel truly alive, but that was beside the point. He'd done it for *her*, and any benefits accruing to him would have been merely accidental.

Still, he knew that reasoning was utterly insane. Ainsley hadn't wanted to marry him only slightly less fervently than she hadn't wanted to marry the Marquess of Cringlewood. She'd made that clear in language so caustic it was a wonder he hadn't been reduced to a pile of smoldering ash.

After Ainsley departed for her great-aunt's manor house a few hours north of Kinglas, Royal had descended into an even gloomier mood alleviated only by drastic amounts of whisky. Fed up, Nick had finally shoved him into the dusty old estate office and ordered him to work. And wonder of wonders, reading through the history of his family and clan had been absorbing. Putting those records in order, watching the ancient story unfold over the centuries, had given Royal a renewed appreciation for his heritage. The proud Kendricks had fought hard for their rightful place in the history of Scotland, and their story was worth remembering.

For a while, the Kendrick sense of pride had even rubbed off on him.

"For all the good it'll do me now," Royal muttered into his teacup.

"What's that?" Nick asked.

Royal waved off the question. "As I said, I was happy to help, especially since it put an end to your incessant nagging."

His brother adopted an air of mild offense. "I never nag anyone. I simply pass on a suggestion now and again."

Victoria choked on her tea.

Nick gently patted her on the back. "Are you all right, sweetheart?"

"Just a little something in my throat," she said as she exchanged amused glances with Royal. Though the Earl of Arnprior always had everyone's best interest in mind, whether the rest of the family agreed with his determination of *best interest* was another matter.

Victoria put down her teacup. "The fact remains that unless we intend to start Royal on the laundry lists, his task has been completed."

"I suppose that's why you've taken up brooding again," Nick said. "Nothing else to occupy your mind."

Except for the debacle with Ainsley was the clear implication.

"You make it sound as though I've made a hobby out of it," Royal said.

"You rather have, dear," Victoria said.

"And you're bloody good at it," Nick wryly added.

Royal mentally winced. "Everyone's got to be good at something."

"You're good at many things," Victoria said. "Besides brooding," she added when Royal lifted a pointed eyebrow.

"Yes," Nick said with an encouraging smile. "You were a fine scholar before your soldiering days. And you've always been the best in the family when it comes to fencing, riding, and training horses. You managed some horses no one else could get near."

"You forgot I was also the best sword dancer in the county," Royal responded dryly. "But my leg prevents me from taking up that mantle again, or training horses for a living. And since I have no intention of burying myself in a library for the foreseeable future, a life of scholarship is out, too."

When Nick and Victoria exchanged another worried look, he sighed. "I'm sorry. I know you're only trying to help. It's just that…"

"You were forced to give up soldiering, which you excelled at," his sister-in-law said. "Believe me, I understand. When I stood accused of murder last year, I was deathly afraid I'd never be able to teach again."

Before she married Nick, Victoria had planned to open her own seminary for young ladies.

"Do you miss teaching?" Royal couldn't help asking.

"Sometimes I do, although I'm fortunate I can still tutor Kade." She flashed her husband a quick smile. "But I found something else to love even more than teaching."

Like her, Royal thought he'd found something new to love—something more important than even his military career. Too bad he'd been wrong about that, too.

Nick raised Victoria's hand to his lips. "Perhaps we'll have a schoolroom full of Kendrick children you can teach someday," he murmured.

She blushed and gave him a shy smile.

"Would you like me to leave the room?" Royal asked politely.

Victoria wrinkled her nose. "Too much?"

"You are rather making me lose my appetite."

She laughed. "Point taken. Let's get back to you."

"On second thought, I think I'd rather see you two act like romantic idiots," Royal said.

"We can do that anytime," Nick said. "Besides, we've been avoiding a discussion of your situation for too long."

Royal eyed his brother with distaste. "You are incredibly annoying."

"If so, it's for your own good. Now, given that you did such a splendid job with my paperwork, I have a suggestion to make."

"Just one?"

Nick, as usual, didn't rise to the bait. "Since we've now uncovered your talent for organization, you should consider working with Logan. You know he'd be thrilled to have your help."

Logan, the second oldest brother, had recently returned to Scotland after years of self-imposed exile in Canada. And now he was rich, owning a successful company trading in fur and timber. Logan was setting up an office and warehouse in Glasgow and had offered a job to any family member who wanted one. Royal had briefly pondered accepting the offer before deciding he'd rather put a bullet through his good leg than spend the rest of his life touting up columns in a dusty warehouse.

"I have no intention of becoming a glorified clerk," he said. "Besides, I'm not much of a city man. After a few weeks in Glasgow, I'm ready to crawl out of my skin."

That feeling had intensified after coming home from the war. The noise, the crowded streets, the bustle and hurry…sometimes he could almost imagine the buildings closing in on him.

"You don't seem particularly enamored with the country these days, either," Nick pointed out.

Royal simply lifted his shoulders in another vague shrug.

Victoria studied him over the rim of her teacup. "Have you heard from Lady Ainsley recently?"

Royal had been about to take another seed cake, but he put down his plate and cautiously regarded his sister-in-law. "No. Why do you ask?"

"Since Glasgow is apparently not to your liking, it might be nice if you made a trip to Cairndow to visit her. The poor girl has been cooped up in that small village for the entire winter with only her great-aunt for company. I'm sure she'd love to see you."

Royal and Nick stared at her as if she'd lost her mind.

"What's wrong with making a little visit?" she asked. "After all, it's less than a day's ride from Kinglas. In fact, I'm quite surprised none of us thought of the idea until now."

"One generally waits for an invitation first," Royal said sarcastically.

"She'd probably shoot you if you showed up at her door unannounced," Nick commented. "You didn't exactly part on the best of terms."

"It wasn't that bad," Royal muttered. Yes, she'd still been furious with him about the failed elopement, but she'd also given him an astonishing, bone-crushing hug before shoving him away and stomping out to her carriage.

"And she *has* written to you over the winter," Victoria pointed out.

Nick glanced at Royal, clearly surprised. "Really? With the exception of Victoria and Kade, she made it clear she thought the rest of us were idiots. Especially you."

"Chuckleheaded nincompoop was her exact description for me," Royal said.

"Then, why—"

The door opened and his grandfather stomped in, sparing Royal the need to explain Ainsley's erratic conduct. He wasn't really sure why she'd written to him, except that she'd sounded rather lonely and bored. But her tone had also made it clear she harbored a lingering irritation with all things Kendrick.

"Ye all look as queer as Dick's hatband," Angus said as joined them at the tea table. "What's afoot?"

"My dear wife has just suggested that Royal visit Lady Ainsley Matthews as a cure for his melancholy," Nick said.

Their grandfather's bushy eyebrows bristled like agitated tomcats. "What? That bloody woman can tear the hide off a man just by lookin' at him— that's if she doesn't stab the puir lad first."

"She's not that bad," Royal said, irritated by his grandfather's somewhat accurate assessment.

"Indeed not," Victoria added. "Lady Ainsley is a lovely girl."

"She's a looker, I'll grant ye," Angus said. "But have ye forgotten her behavior on the elopement? Because I have not." He directed his scowl at Royal. "Her high and mightiness treated us like muck on her boot heel."

"Of course I remember. I was there, wasn't I?"

It was *all* etched in Royal's mind with hideous clarity. In addition to Ainsley, his grandfather, and his idiot twin brothers, Royal had been dealing with two other young ladies from Glasgow who the twins had been courting for several weeks. The lasses had initially been enthusiastic elopement participants.

Ainsley, however, had not been willing, and Royal had completely misread her. After he scooped her up that fateful night and dumped her into his carriage, she'd exploded in a fury of thrashing arms and legs, all but unmanning him. Fortunately, her foot had landed on his bad thigh instead of an even worse spot. Royal had practically passed out from the pain, but at least it had brought her up short.

Once he'd recovered himself, he'd explained the plan to a still furious Ainsley. She had then surprised him by declining his offer to return to Glasgow, saying she'd rather be ruined forever than marry the Marquess of Cringlewood. An aborted elopement with Royal, she'd decided, would be enough to generate the sort of scandal necessary to ruin her reputation and convince Cringlewood to leave her alone.

She'd then spent the rest of the trip north ordering his family about like a bunch of lazy servants and fighting almost constantly with Angus.

"One can hardly blame her for being angry," Royal said. "After all, I did kidnap her."

"And then subjected her to three horrible days caring for a castle full of sick people," Victoria replied in a humorous tone. "It's a miracle she didn't shove you off the battlements as repayment."

On top of everything else, one of the twins had slipped off the coach step and broken a leg on the way to Kinglas. After their arrival home, half the family and staff had promptly come down with a severe cold, pitching the entire household into chaos. Nick and Victoria, who'd followed the elopers in hot pursuit, had ably managed the crisis with assistance from Royal and—surprisingly—Ainsley, who'd turned out to be a rather competent nurse.

"Angus, even you must admit Lady Ainsley acquitted herself well under the circumstances," Victoria said.

"I'll give ye that," the old man grudgingly acknowledged. "The lass did better than I expected. But I still say she's a *Sassenach* harridan, and our Royal shouldna have anything to do with the likes of her."

Victoria shook her head. "I'm concerned about her. She said a few things while she was here that quite worried me. I regret I didn't have the opportunity to follow up on them."

"You were too busy getting arrested for murder," Royal said, "so I think you can be excused for the oversight."

Nick frowned. "The less said about that incident, the better. I will not have anyone upsetting my wife with reminders of that exceedingly unpleasant time."

"Yes, dear," Victoria said in soothing tones, patting his arm. "Although everything did turn out for the best, so all's well that end's well."

Nick's mouth quirked up. "Now you're just managing me, love."

"She manages all of us, in case you haven't noticed," Royal said. "Which is a good thing, since we cause more trouble than we're worth."

"Speak for yerself," Angus said in a lofty tone. "I'm a paragon compared to the lot of ye."

"If you're a paragon, then I'm Robert the Bruce," Royal said. "And I do believe I left my crown in the drawing room. Will you fetch it for me, Grandda?"

Angus bristled with indignation. "Now, see here, laddie—"

Nick interrupted the impending Angus Eruption. "We've wandered some distance from the original topic of Royal's future. He cannot spend his time moping around Kinglas. He needs to find something useful to do with his life."

"Well, I'll not be thankin' ye to give him any more of *my* work," the old man said. "Ye'll not be puttin' me out to pasture just yet."

Their grandfather was understandably touchy, on the lookout for any hint that he wasn't contributing to the family's wellbeing or was in any way a burden. Royal knew exactly how he felt.

"It's just that Royal seems at loose ends," Victoria explained. "We're trying to decide how best to address the situation."

"And do I actually get a say?" Royal asked sardonically.

They ignored him.

"Running aboot after that stuck-up English miss is the last thing he should be doin'," Angus said. "Besides, I doubt she'd even see him."

Royal thought about Ainsley's last letter to him a few weeks ago, the one where she'd sounded...sad. "Actually, I'm not sure she'd mind a visit."

Nick put down his teacup and stood. "You'll make your own decision, of course. But I would be grateful if you would at least consider working for Logan."

"And ye'll no be turnin' the lad into a glorified clerk, either," Angus objected. "He'll be stayin' right here at Kinglas, where he belongs."

His grandfather meant where he could keep an eye on him, since he constantly feared Royal might suffer a relapse of some sort or the other.

"It'll be fine, Grandda," Royal said. "Don't fash yourself."

"Of course I get fashed," Angus said gruffly. "After all, ye almost died fightin' for the stupid English."

"Ahem," Victoria said loudly.

Nick clamped a hand on the old man's shoulder. "Come along, Grandda. I want to take a look at the south wall of the stables. It might even need rebuilding, and I'd like your opinion."

"Of course, lad," Angus said, instantly diverted. "I've been thinkin' the same myself."

"Then let's get to it." Nick started to propel Angus toward the door.

"Laddie, don't be makin' any plans without talkin' to me first," the old man called to Royal before he disappeared.

"Thank God," Victoria said with a sigh. "I do love the old fellow, but sometimes he can be such a trial."

"But you manage him exceedingly well."

"As much as Angus *can* be managed. I admit that sometimes I'm tempted to clobber him with his own bagpipes."

When Royal laughed, Victoria gave him a relieved smile. "The discussion was getting rather fraught, wasn't it? I'm sorry we made such a fuss. I know you hate it."

"A fuss is entirely unnecessary, I assure you. I'm perfectly well."

A moment later, his youngest brother came rushing into the library.

"Nick just told me Taffy made seed cakes," Kade said as he plopped down next to Victoria on the settee. "Oh, good. You saved me some." He promptly crammed one into his mouth.

"Dear, there's no need to wolf it down," Victoria said, handing the lad a plate and a serviette. "Remember your manners."

Royal leaned over and ruffled his brother's hair. "If you're not careful, someone will mistake you for one of the twins."

"Taffy hardly *ever* makes seed cakes, so you can't blame me. And Graeme and Grant aren't nearly as bad-mannered as they used to be," Kade said around a mouthful.

"Swallow before talking, please," Victoria admonished.

"The twins have become marginally civilized thanks to you, Victoria," Royal said. "We were all barbarians until you came along."

"Oh, you weren't that bad," Victoria said.

"Oh, yes, we were."

She grinned. "All right, the twins and Angus were quite appalling at first, and you were only slightly less objectionable. I still have nightmares about my first days at Kinglas. Kade, though, was perfect from the outset."

The boy leaned affectionately against her shoulder, throwing Royal a smug glance that made him laugh. It was grand to see Kade doing so well after years of ill health and suffering.

"What were you talking about when I came in?" Kade asked, reaching for another cake.

Victoria hesitated, eyeing Royal. He shrugged.

"We were discussing whether your brother might like to visit Lady Ainsley," she said.

Kade fastened an earnest gaze on Royal. "So, why don't you?"

Royal waggled a hand. "I'm not entirely sure she'd want to see me."

"She would," Kade said before biting into his seed cake.

"You're sure about that, are you?" Royal asked dryly.

After swallowing another enormous bite, his brother nodded. "I think Lady Ainsley likes you. A lot."

Royal ignored the jolt to his heart. "She certainly liked to scold me."

Kade shook his head. "She didn't mean it. It was just her way of dealing with you. Sometimes you can be quite gruff, you know. So she pushes back."

"Kade's opinion makes a great deal of sense," Victoria said.

Royal thought so too. Although only fifteen, Kade had a perception that was beyond his years and probably greater than the rest of the Kendrick males put together.

"Besides," the boy added, "I like her, because Lady Ainsley always says exactly what she means. Adults usually don't."

"She's honest, I'll give you that," Royal said.

"Regardless of your rather fraught past with Lady Ainsley," Victoria said, "I agree with Kade. She might have trouble admitting it, but I'm sure the girl is very fond of you."

He'd been sure of that at one point, too, and look where it had got him.

"Maybe," he said in a neutral tone.

"If nothing else, she's your friend," Victoria said. "And I have the feeling she could use a friend right now."

"Even one of us blasted Kendricks?"

"One Kendrick in particular," she said firmly.

He finally allowed himself to seriously consider the idea. Seeing Ainsley again would be a challenge. They were often like two comets colliding, generating a good deal of heat, noise, and smoke. They also tended to leave a pile of rubble in their wake, which was not pleasant for anyone who happened to be within the blast range.

More to the point, Royal couldn't figure out what she wanted from him. More than once she'd come to him, as if needing comfort and protection, but then she'd pushed him away and claimed she never wanted to see him again. The confounded girl was as mysterious as the bloody Sphinx.

Then again, she *had* written to him three times this winter, hadn't she?

Victoria's gaze was astute. "You will never know how she feels unless you ask her directly."

"She'll probably demonstrate her feelings by smashing a vase over my head."

"That is a distinct possibility, I admit," said Victoria. "But whether she is worth the risk is a question only you can answer."

"Lady A has my vote," said Kade, "despite what anyone else says about her. She's a corker, if you ask me."

Clearly, a second Kendrick male had fallen under the spell of Ainsley Matthews's considerable charms. And since the lad *was* probably the smartest of them all…

"As it so happens, little brother, I agree with you." Royal hauled himself to his feet, a surge of unfamiliar energy coursing through his body. "Now, if you'll excuse me, I must pack a bag for my trip."

"Oh, good," Kade said, reaching for the tea tray. "More cake for me."

***

More info, excerpts, and buy links on Vanessa's website: https://www.vanessakellyauthor.com/book s/the-highlander-who-protected-me/

ABOUT VANESSA KELLY

Named by *Booklist* as one of the "New Stars of Historical Romance," USA Today Bestselling author **Vanessa Kelly**'s books have been nominated for awards in a number of contests. She is also the recipient of the prestigious Maggie Medallion for historical romance. With a Master's Degree in English Literature, Vanessa is known for developing vibrant Regency settings, appealing characters, and witty storylines that captivate readers. You can visit her on the web at vanessakellyauthor.com. Be sure to join her mailing list for exclusive content and contests.

MORE BOOKS BY VANESSA KELLY

THE HIGHLANDER WHO PROTECTED ME (Clan Kendrick 1), Oct. 2018:
https://www.vanessakellyauthor.com/books/the-highlander-who-protected-me/

THE HIGHLANDER'S PRINCESS BRIDE (Improper Princesses 3), out now:
https://www.vanessakellyauthor.com/books/the-highlanders-princess-bride/

THREE WEEKS WITH A PRINCESS (Improper Princesses 2), out now:
http://www.vanessakellyauthor.com/books/three-weeks-with-a-princess/

MY FAIR PRINCESS: (Improper Princesses 1), out now:
http://www.vanessakellyauthor.com/books/my-fair-princess/

The Renegade Royals Series:
http://www.vanessakellyauthor.com/books/

The Stanton Family Series:
http://www.vanessakellyauthor.com/books/

Made in the USA
Middletown, DE
25 September 2020